Winter of Artifice

Three Novelettes

Winter of Artifice

Three Novelettes

Anaïs Nin

With engravings by Ian Hugo

Introduction by Laura Frost

SWALLOW PRESS / OHIO UNIVERSITY PRESS

ATHENS, OHIO

Swallow Press
An imprint of Ohio University Press, Athens, Ohio 45701
ohioswallow.com

Printed in the United States of America
Swallow Press / Ohio University Press books are printed on acid-free paper ⊗ ™

26 25 24 23 22 21 20 19 18 17 16   5 4 3 2 1

Library of Congress Control Number: 2016957353

Contents

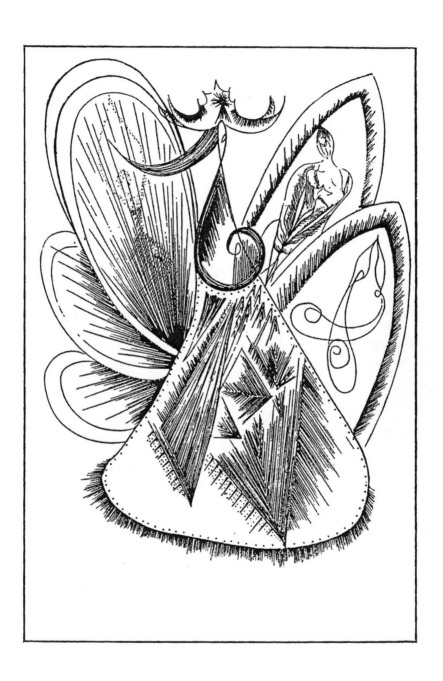

Introduction

Laura Frost

Long before *Fifty Shades of Grey* and the women's erotica boom, before "chick lit" such as *Bridget Jones* and *Sex and the City*, before *Eat Pray Love* and the memoir craze, there was Anaïs Nin. As a first-person chronicler of a woman's experiences of selfhood, love, creativity, and sexuality, Nin stands alone. Yet even as her works have influenced generations of writers, literary history has not been kind to her. Today Nin is typically regarded as a minor or cult author best known for her collections of sexy short stories (*Three Little Birds, Delta of Venus*) and, even more so, for her epic, twelve-volume diary charting her path during two world wars, through Paris in the 1920s and '30s, Greenwich Village in the '40s, and Los Angeles in the '60s, amid many of the century's most innovative artistic, literary, and intellectual circles.

The diary is also the source of Nin's reputation as a narcissist with a tenuous relationship to the truth and as a compulsive seductress with a shaky social conscience and even shakier ethics. The posthumous publication of unexpurgated volumes of Nin's diary came with revelations about her sex life, including the explicit details of her affairs with writer Henry Miller and his wife June, as well as with two of Nin's famous therapists, all audaciously recounted in juicy prose (e.g., Nin's self-declared "recipe for happiness" at a time she was conducting multiple liaisons was to "mix well the sperm of four men in one day"[1]).

Critics excoriated Nin for her overblown prose, her constant deception of loved ones (she was, for a period, secretly married to two men at the same time), a string of seemingly cavalier abortions, including a harrowingly late-term one, and an affair with her father when she was an adult. Subsequent biographies and articles capitalized on the irony that an author who purported to tell all should seem to have been hiding so much.[2]

If, as Nin's biographer Deirdre Bair observes, Nin "has fallen into disrepute" because of her so-called "liary," her fiction has been even more neglected.[3] While Nin's poetry, stories, and novels have been embraced by many readers, she has often been faulted for her solipsistic and undisciplined style and for her insular, apolitical tendencies, as she seemed to be oblivious to the tumultuous historical and political events of her day.[4] Moreover, while Nin was always searching for a distinctive female voice and benefited from a feminist fan base, she was not an activist.[5]

The reissue of *Winter of Artifice* presents an opportunity for a renewed assessment of Nin's contributions. A collection of three novellas about women navigating urban landscapes and looking inward at their own psyches as "cities of the interior" (as Nin would call a subsequent group of her novels), *Winter of Artifice* feels, even more than sixty years later, quite contemporary. It begins with a cinema starlet contemplating her image on the screen and ends in a psychoanalyst's office in a Manhattan skyscraper as he counsels patients who are baffled by modern life. "I have depicted the malady of today's soul," Nin remarked about *Winter of Artifice* in her diary.[6] Her writing in these novellas is surreal, impressionistic, and fragmented, but also bold, with lyrical, poetic passages. *Winter of Artifice* corrects the notion that Nin was an eccentric one-off. Rather, her work has to be considered as taking part in artistic and even philosophical traditions of modernism (the period roughly between World Wars I and II, including authors such as James Joyce, Virginia Woolf, William Faulkner, and Jean Rhys), literary confession, and memoir, as well as narratives of transgressive sexuality.

And the question of literary legacy works forward as well. Nin paved the way for controversial contemporary memoirs such as

Kathryn Harrison's *The Kiss*, Catherine Millet's *The Sexual Life of Catherine M.*, and Toni Bentley's *The Surrender*, as well as bravura literary performances like Karl Ove Knausgaard's six-volume *My Struggle*, with its hyperdetailed focus on the minutiae of one man's life.[7] Without falsely elevating Nin's craftsmanship or exaggerating the profundity of her insights, the moment is right to consider her work in the context of other experimental writers of her time and also from our present vantage point, where the kinds of literature Nin helped pioneer have only recently achieved serious commercial success and critical attention.

The Winter of Artifice was first published in 1939, in a form substantially different from that of the present volume.[8] At that time, Nin complained about critics who read it as autobiography.[9] Actually, the two are inextricably linked, as Nin routinely transposed material from her diary into her fiction, reworking it but retaining striking resemblances to the original source. To note that with Nin all roads lead to her diary is not to fault her but rather to recognize her distinct approach. One of the primary reasons she started therapy was because she felt she was unable to break out of her autobiographical mode and write fiction. One could argue that she never really did, but rather forged a hybrid model that mixed fiction and memoir. Since *Winter of Artifice* is no exception, it is necessary to start with its genesis in Nin's diary.

* * *

Born in France in 1903 to a Spanish composer/pianist father and a French-Danish singer mother, Nin began her diary at the age of eleven when she sailed with her mother and brothers from Barcelona to New York. Reeling from her father's recent abandonment of the family, she conceived of the diary as an unsent letter to him.[10] Nin writes of a character in *Winter of Artifice* whose history closely parallels her own, "Only in her diary could she reveal her true self, her true feelings. What she really desired was to be left alone with her diary and her dreams of her father."[11] Diary writing quickly became a compulsion—one of her therapists would liken it to an opium addiction[12]—as Nin assiduously recorded the details of her life, including her decision in her youth to earn a living as a writer, her marriage to a banker, Hugh Guiler, who financially supported her (and her lovers, unknowingly), and, of course, her vigorous sex life.

From very early on, Nin thought of her diary as a crafted literary work and wrote with a sense of an audience beyond herself. She always said that rather than aiming to achieve realism (that is, a faithful transcription of objective events), she sought to capture "psychological reality," or the way the mind perceives and experiences the world, which she thought was infinitely richer than realism. "In fiction," she commented in *The Novel of the Future*, "I dwell on the pursuit of the hidden self. I give much importance to the Walter Mitty in all of us, to our dreams and fantasies. . . . The external story is what I consider unreal."[13] These comments are relevant for her fiction and her diary alike. Both dwell on the characters' internal states rather than the external story, the subjective rather than the objective dimension.

Like many experimental writers of the period, Nin had difficulty finding a commercial publisher for her writing. "All strategic points in literature are held by little men," she griped in her diary after a frustrating meeting with a book critic.[14] In recent years, scholars of early twentieth-century literature have celebrated the small, independent presses and magazines that supported innovative writing, yet the two presses that Nin started are rarely recognized. Nin's first work of fiction, *The House of Incest*, was self-published in 1936 by a Paris-based press, Siana ("Anaïs" backwards), that she formed with Henry Miller and another writer, Michael Fraenkel. Her next volume of fiction, originally titled *The Winter of Artifice*, featuring three stories ("Djuna," "Lilith," and "The Voice"), was issued in 1939 by the Obelisk Press, Jack Kahane's legendary imprint that published a mixture of pornography and "literary" works such as Miller's *Tropic of Cancer*, Radclyffe Hall's groundbreaking novel of lesbian desire, *Well of Loneliness*, and Lawrence Durrell's *Black Book*.

The Winter of Artifice debuted a week before the start of World War II. Discouraged by the book's lack of impact and limited distribution, Nin bought a printing press when she moved to New York in the 1940s and installed it in her Greenwich Village studio, christening the project Gemor Press (an allusion to one of her lovers).

She handset a new version of the book, now including only two stories ("Stella" and "Winter of Artifice") rather than the present three.[15] In her diary, Nin describes the revision as both aesthetic and physical: "I have not spared my hands. My nails are broken. I have not spared my book. I have slashed into its imperfections. It is shorter, better focused."[16] Three years later, in 1945, Swallow Press published yet another version of *Winter of Artifice,* expanded again to the three stories that correspond to the contents of the present volume and featuring illustrations by Guiler, under the pseudonym Ian Hugo.

The idea of a book under constant revision and transformation mirrors Nin's preoccupation with identity in constant flux, with the concept of a multiplicity of selves within each person, and also with the inherent theatricality of the self. These themes are foregrounded in the opening of *Winter of Artifice,* in the story "Stella": an actress sits "in a small, dark room and watched her own figure acting on the screen. Stella watched her 'double' moving in the light, and she did not recognize her" (1). The actress, Nin suggests, undergoes an only more pronounced version of the self-estrangement that all modern people experience.

Stella ("star" in Italian) lives in a "movie star apartment" (14) with a "very large, very spacious Movie Star bed of white satin" and a glamorous wardrobe including hats and shoes she is too intimidated to wear (3–4). Stella embarks on a dalliance with a married man named Bruno; they repeatedly experience misunderstandings, looking to one another with impossible expectations. Meanwhile, Stella's father, a stage actor and a compulsive liar, asks her to help him reconcile with his lover, to whom he has been unfaithful. Even though Stella resents her father's philandering ways, she replicates them.

What is missing from this cursory summary of "Stella" is everything that makes the story distinct: the style of Nin's prose, its fragmentation, the way she structures the scenes, abruptly moving from one place and time to another without any explanatory details in between. Like her heroes D. H. Lawrence, Henry Miller, and other modernists such as James Joyce, Virginia Woolf, Mina Loy, Antonin Artaud, and Marcel Proust, Nin was dissatisfied with the literary forms she had inherited. "The pure novel," she wrote in her diary, "can only reveal a static fragment, freeze it, when the truth is not in that particular fragment but in continuous change. The novel arbitrarily chooses a moment in time, a segment. Frames it. Binds it."[17] Throughout *Winter of Artifice*, plot is secondary to the fluctuations of the characters' inner states, feelings, conflicts, and anxieties as Nin strives to capture the *lived* texture of psychological and emotional life, rather than an artificial reproduction of the external world.[18]

"Stella" articulates one woman's relationship to her inner and outer selves; it is also, at the same time, a meditation on the latest art form, cinema. Films had only recently shifted from the silents to the talkies, and Nin saw cinema as a medium even more significant than her own, arguing that "it was not the writers but the filmmakers who opened the way to the language of images which is the language of the unconscious."[19] Nin was an enthusiastic spectatrix of films from her teens onward. She appeared in the experimental filmmaker Maya Deren's film *Ritual in Transfigured Time* (1946), as well as her husband's *Bells of Atlantis* (in which Nin reads a passage from *House of Incest*) and Kenneth Anger's *Inauguration of the Pleasure Dome* (1954). Nin's interest in film went beyond fandom: she even suggested that her fiction had been influenced by cinematic techniques like jump cuts, flashbacks, and an emphasis on image over dialogue.[20] In "Stella," then, the form of the writing matches the subject matter, as Nin draws inspiration from the screen. One sign of the story's à la mode qualities was its publication in the August 1946 edition of the chic journal *Harper's Bazaar*, which at the time featured quality fiction by Virginia Woolf, F. Scott and Zelda Fitzgerald, Anita Loos (*Harper's* serialized her novel *Gentlemen Prefer Blondes*), Mary McCarthy, and Dorothy Parker, among other established and emerging authors. The accompanying author photograph was a still from Nin's cameo in Deren's film.[21]

In the second story in *Winter of Artifice,* a woman who has been waiting for her father for twenty years is at last reunited with him. They are intoxicated with one another. He tells her, "Although I was prevented from training you, your blood obeyed me. . . . Now I see that all these women I pursued are all in you, and you are my daughter, and I can't marry you! You are the synthesis of all the women I loved" (59). This drama of recognition and misrecognition between the father and the daughter culminates in several italicized pages of anguished archetypes and erotic imagery, such as violin bows drawn between legs, that together insinuate a sexual encounter (60–62).

A daughter becoming "the mystical bride of her father" violates the strongest of social taboos; the episode is all the more startling given that Nin recapitulates the episode from her diary: "He and I should not have tried to meet in life," she wrote of her rendezvous with her father, "but in some strange region of dreamlike frozenness. We were punished for trying to materialize a myth. . . . See *Winter of Artifice* for development of theme."[22]

On that note, although Nin's writing is sometimes considered a model of sensitive feminine subjectivity, her work—and especially her diary—is also a document of sexual conquest comparable to those of male libertines such as the Marquis de Sade, Casanova, Frank Harris, or Klaus Kinski. When Nin wrote about her erotic life, it was pronounced solipsistic smut; when men did it, it was cast in a tradition of literary transgression. Nin knew the legacy of erotic writing—she comments on, for example, the surrealist writer Georges Bataille (*Story of the Eye*) and decadent writer Leopold von Sacher-Masoch (*Venus in Furs*) in her diaries— and she deliberately created her own place within it, even in the erotica that she wrote for an anonymous pornography collector for the rate of a dollar a page.

Significantly, Nin's first published book was a volume of literary criticism, *D. H. Lawrence: An Unprofessional Study* (1932). When Lawrence died in March 1930, he was regarded primarily as a writer of racy novels (e.g., *Women in Love, Lady Chatterley's Lover*) that were censored during his lifetime; Lawrence saw himself as a sort of social prophet striving to rejuvenate what he saw as deadened and jaded postwar culture by reinvigorating the way people thought about sex. Like other—mainly male—writers of the time, Lawrence saw the exploration of hitherto taboo aspects of sexuality as one of his central projects and sought to push the boundaries of sexual expression and representation. Nin was inspired by Lawrence's belief in the power of sexuality in shaping human—and especially feminine—experience.

The final section of *Winter of Artifice,* "The Voice," offers an initial reprieve from the intense, suffocating father-daughter stories of "Stella" and "Winter." As if pulling a camera away from a close-up for a wider angle, Nin sets "The Voice" in "the tallest hotel in the City, in a building shooting upward like a railroad track set for the moon. A million rooms like cells, all exactly alike" (87). Into this metropolitan vision pour people who are "struggling, defeated, wounded, crippled" and "feverishly eager to confess" to a modern-day priest: a psychoanalyst, who is referred to throughout the story as "the Voice" (88, 87). Here the self is given a new setting—the therapy session—as the Voice's patients share their fantasies, dreams, and free associations.

"The Voice" illustrates how powerfully Nin was influenced by surrealism, the avant-garde artistic movement in the 1920s and '30s that explored the subconscious and irrational mind in art. While it could seem to detractors as if surrealists such as Salvador Dalí and André Breton were creating their art by random processes, they did, in fact, have deliberate methods. By promoting automatic writing, states of reverie, and dreams, and by ripping words and objects out of their everyday contexts and allowing the play of coincidence, surrealism sought to liberate the imagination and desire, however strange and disturbing. Nin combined this sensibility with Freud's so-called talking cure (psychoanalysis), which encouraged free association, to sketch the minds of her restless characters. Djuna, the first patient, tells the Voice, "I stand for hours watching the river downtown. What obsesses me is the debris . . . Punctured rubber dolls bobbing up and down like foetuses . . . Dead cats. Corks. Bread that looks like entrails. . . . These things haunt me" (88). Her monologue unfolds in a torrent of tawdry images that seem to mix reality and fantasy. Like Nin's diary, the lost and confused patients' outpourings to the Voice represent their psychological reality, the conflicted terrain of inner life.

To be sure, the world of *Winter of Artifice* is one of misery, dysfunction, and anxiety. One of Nin's literary models for this moodiness was the 1936 novel *Nightwood* by the American modernist Djuna Barnes (Nin even wrote Barnes a fan letter). Set in bohemian Paris, *Nightwood* follows a turbulent lesbian love affair; the women wander in urban labyrinths of tortured desire among characters including a cross-dressing doctor and a tattooed circus artist, all alienated and unsettled. *Winter of Artifice* brings to mind the meditative prose and heavy, claustrophobic atmosphere of *Nightwood* as well as its dark world of abject people begging a hapless doctor to help reconcile them to their desires, fantasies, fears, and shame.

While Barnes's novel may seem to be a hermetic, self-referential universe, it has also been interpreted as an indirect response to the frightening politics of the moment, with the disenfranchised characters analogous to the targets of fascism.[23] Nin seemed to have had a similar approach in mind. "While I finish printing *Winter of Artifice*," she writes in her diary, "the nightmare of the world grows immense, a chamber of horrors, a tortured world, bigger than I can bear to encompass. . . . Surely one has to create against this. One has to build private shelters against this not to be contaminated or maddened by it."[24] Through the intimate worlds of *Winter of Artifice,* Nin renders the horror of history as persistent psychic disturbance. Cruelty in these stories comes from a lack of self-knowledge inflicted on others that is repeated in a chain of violence. Introspection, then, and the project of knowing oneself might have an effect beyond a "private shelter." Part of the originality of Barnes, Nin, Jean Rhys, and others who created fictions that tunnel into characters' private worlds was that they did so at a time writers were being asked to be overtly politically engaged.

If for Nin artistic creation is one bulwark against the horrors of history, the study of the self—whether through the "talking cure" of analysis or unflinching self reflection—is another. *Winter of Artifice* suggests that self-reflection and self-study are a means of examining and perhaps overcoming what Nin called "the violence and brutality of modern life."[25] That she consistently grounded her project so deeply in her own self was provocative and novel. Nin's flouting of the convention that we subordinate (or at least disguise) our narcissism and "take an interest in others," and her transgression of sexual and social mores, remain as singular today as in her own time.

* * *

Nin contributed a body of work tracking the vicissitudes of modern psychology that remains unmatched. Many of the problems that her writing addresses remain unanswered: for example, the latitude allowed for artistic fabrication/invention in texts that purport to be autobiography (the outrage about James Frey's *A Million Little Pieces* is only one of many episodes arising from this issue); how an author's behavior or character affects our reading of his/her work; and, perhaps most centrally, the nature of the interface between inner life and the external world. "I have entered the dream with a powerful beam of light," Nin noted of *Winter of Artifice* in her diary, "to interpret, reveal its influence on our life, to focus on its influence, and the interdependence of fantasy and reality."[26] We are still struggling to understand the "interdependence of fantasy and reality," especially in terms of women's sexuality. Nin, libertine, adventurer, spectator of the self, mistress of disguise and transformation, still has something to tell us.

NOTES

1. Deirdre Bair, *Anaïs Nin: A Biography* (New York: G. P. Putnam's Sons, 1995), 169.

2. For a sense of the critical reception of Nin's posthumous work see, for example, Carol Anshaw, "Anaïs Nin: Many Words, Many Lovers and a Host of Lies," *Chicago Tribune*, October 24, 1993 (http://articles.chicagotribune.com/1993-10-24/entertainment/9310240069_1_otto-rank-noel-riley-fitch-Anaïs-nin); Miranda Seymour, "Sex, Lies, and Narcissism," *Independent*, May 20, 1995 (http://www.independent.co.uk/arts-entertainment/books/sex-lies-and-narcissism-1620319.html); and "The Truth Wasn't Sexy Enough," *New York Times*, October 17, 1993, also by Seymour (http://www.nytimes.com/1993/10/17/books/truth-wasn-t-sexy-enough.html).

3. Bair, xviii.

4. See Marion N. Fay's summary of how Nin's reputation with feminist critics and scholars has changed over time, in *Anaïs Nin's*

Narratives, ed. Anne T. Salvatore (Gainesville: University Press of Florida, 2001), 38; and also Shari Benstock's *Women of the Left Bank: Paris, 1900–1940* (Austin: University of Texas Press, 1986), 424.

5. Anaïs Nin, "Notes on Feminism," *Massachusetts Review* 13, no. 1/2 (Winter–Spring 1972): 25–28.

6. Anaïs Nin, *The Diary of Anaïs Nin*, vol. 3, *1939–1944*, ed. Gunther Stuhlmann (New York: Harcourt Brace & World, 1969), 194.

7. Kathryn Harrison, *The Kiss* (New York: Random House, 1997); Catherine Millett, *The Sexual Life of Catherine M.*, trans. Adriana Hunter (New York: Grove Press, 2002); Toni Bentley, *The Surrender: An Erotic Memoir* (New York: Ecco, 2004); and Karl Ove Knausgaard, *My Struggle*, vol. 1, trans. Don Bartlett (New York: Farrar Straus Giroux, 2013).

8. Anaïs Nin, *The Winter of Artifice*, facsimile of the original 1939 Paris edition (Troy, MI: Sky Blue Press, 2007).

9. Nin, *Diary*, 3:204–5.

10. Bair, 29.

11. Nin, *Winter of Artifice* (Athens: Swallow Press, 2016), 43. Hereafter, page references to this edition are cited parenthetically in the text.

12. Nin's account of Otto Rank's comment appears in her unpublished papers in the UCLA collection. Qtd. by Bair, 189.

13. Nin, *The Novel of the Future* (Athens, OH: Swallow Press, 2014), 45.

14. Bair, 190.

15. For more on the history of the different versions, see http://anaisninblog.skybluepress.com/tag/the-winter-of-artifice/, accessed April 17, 2015.

16. Nin, *Diary*, 3:194.

17. Ibid.

18. Nin, *The Novel of the Future*, 3.

19. Ibid., 97.

20. Wendy M. DuBow, ed., *Conversations with Anaïs Nin* (Jackson: University Press of Mississippi, 1994), 203–4. See also "The Actress and the Femme Fatale," in Helen Tookey's *Anaïs Nin, Fictionality and Femininity: Playing a Thousand Roles* (New York: Oxford University Press, 2003).

21. Benjamin Franklin and Duane Schneider, *Anaïs Nin: An Introduction* (Athens, OH: Ohio University Press, 1979), 21.

22. *The Diary of Anaïs Nin*, vol. 1, *1931–1934*, ed. Gunther Stuhlmann (New York: Harcourt Brace Jovanovich, 1966), 308.

23. Jane Marcus, "Laughing at Leviticus: *Nightwood* as Woman's Circus Epic," in *Silence and Power: A Reevaluation of Djuna Barnes*, ed. Mary Lynn Broe (Carbondale: Southern Illinois University Press, 1991), 221–51.

24. Nin, *Diary*, 3:195.

25. Ibid., 194.

26. Ibid.

Winter of Artifice

Three Novelettes

Stella

STELLA sat in a small, dark room and watched her own figure acting on the screen. Stella watched her "double" moving in the light, and she did not recognize her. She almost hated her. Her first reaction was one of revolt, of rejection. This image was not she. She repudiated it. It was a work of artifice, of lighting, of stage setting.

The shock she felt could not be explained by the obvious difference between her daily self to which she purposely brought no enhancement and the screen image which was illuminated. It was not only that the eyes were enlarged and deepened, that the long eyelashes played like some Oriental latticework around them and intensified the interior light. The shock came from some violent contrast between Stella's image of herself and the projected self she could not recognize at all. To begin with, she had always seen herself in her own interior mirror, as a child woman, too small. And then this little bag of poison she carried within, the poison of melancholy and dissatisfaction she always felt must be apparent in her coloring, must produce a grey tone, or brown (the colors she wore in preference to others, the sackcloth robes of punishment). And the paralyzing fears, fear of love, fear of people coming too near (nearness brings wounds), invading her—her tensions and stage frights in the face of love. . . . The first kiss for example, that first kiss which was to transport her, dissolve her, which was to swing her upward into the only paradise on earth . . . that first kiss of which she had been so frightened that at the moment of the miracle, out of panic, nerves, from her delicately shaped stomach came dark rumbling like some long-sleeping volcano becoming active.

Whereas the image on the screen was completely washed of the coloring and tones of sadness. It was imponderably light, and moved always with such a flowering of gestures that it was like the bloom and flowering of nature. This figure moved with ease, with illimitableness towards others, in a dissolution of feeling. The eyes opened and all the marvels of love, all its tonalities and nuances and multiplicities poured out as for a feast. The body danced a dance of receptivity and response. The hair undulated and swung as if it had

1

breathing pores of its own, its own currents of life and electricity, and the hands preceded the gesture of the body like some slender orchestra leader's baton unleashing a symphony.

This was not the grey-faced child who had run away from home to become an actress, who had known hunger and limitations and obstacles, who had not yet given herself as she was giving herself on the screen. . . .

And the second shock was the response of the people.

They loved her.

Sitting next to her, they did not see her, intent on loving the woman on the screen.

Because she was giving to many what most gave to the loved one. A voice altered by love, desire, the lips forming a smile of open tenderness. They were permitted to witness the exposure of being in a moment of high feeling, of tenderness, indulgence, dreaming, abandon, sleepiness, mischievousness, which was only uncovered in moments of love and intimacy.

They received these treasures of a caressing glance, a unique tonality and voice, an intimate gesture by which we are enchanted and drawn to the one we love. This openness they were sharing was the miraculous openness and revelation which took place only in love, and it caused a current of love to flow between the audience and the woman on the screen, a current of gratitude. . . . Then this response moved like a searchlight and found her, smaller, less luminous, less open, poorer, and like some diminished image of the other, but it flowed around her, identified her. The audience came near her, touched her, asked for her signature. And she hung her head, drooped, could not accept the worship. The woman on the screen was a stranger to her. She did not see any analogy, she saw only the violent contrast which only reinforced her conviction that the screen image was illusory, artificial, artful. She was a deceiver, a pretender. The woman on the screen went continually forward, carried by her story, led by the plot loaned to her. But Stella, Stella herself was blocked over and and over again by inner obstacles.

What Stella had seen on the screen, the figure of which she had been so instantaneously jealous, was the free Stella. What did not appear on the screen was the shadow of Stella, her demons, doubt and fear. And Stella was jealous. She was not only jealous of a more beautiful woman, but of a free woman. She marvelled at her own movements, their flow and ease. She marvelled at the passionate giving that came like a flood from her eyes, melting everyone, an act of osmosis. And it was to this woman men wrote letters and this woman they fell in love with, courted.

They courted the face on the screen, the face of translucence, the face of wax on which men found it possible to imprint the image of their fantasy.

No metallic eyes or eyes of crystal as in other women, but liquid, throwing a mist dew and vapor. No definite smile but a hovering, evanescent, uncapturable smile which set off all pursuits. An air of the unformed, waiting to be formed, an air of eluding, waiting to be crystallized, an air of evasion, waiting to be catalyzed. Indefinite contours, a wavering voice capable of all tonalities, tapering to a whisper, an air of flight waiting to be captured, an air of turning corners perpetually and vanishing, some quality of matter that calls for an imprint, a carving, this essence of the feminine on which men could impose any desire, which awaited fecundation, which invited, lured, appealed, drew, ensorcelled by its seeming incompleteness, its hazy mysteries, its rounded edges.

The screen Stella with her transparent wax face, changing and changeable, promising to meet any desire, to mould itself, to respond, to invent if necessary . . . so that the dream of man like some sharp instrument knew the moment had come to imprint his most secret image . . . The image of Stella mobile, receiving the wish, the desire, the image imposed upon it.

She bought a very large, very spacious Movie Star bed of white satin.

It was not the bed of her childhood, which was particularly small because her father had said she was a pixie and she would never grow taller.

It was not the student bed on which she had slept during the years of poverty before she became a well-known actress.

It was the bed she had dreamed and placed in a setting of grandeur, it was the bed that her screen self had often been placed in, very wide and very sumptuous and not like her at all. And together

3

with the bed she had dreamed a room of mirrors, and very large perfume bottles and a closet full of hats and rows of shoes, and the white rug and setting of a famous screen actress, altogether as it had been dreamed by so many women. And finally she had them all, and she lived among them without feeling that they belonged to her, that she had the stature and the assurance they demanded. The large bed . . . she slept in it as if she were sleeping in a screen story. Uneasily. And not until she found a way of slipping her small body away from the splendor, satin, space, did she sleep well: by covering her head.

And when she covered her head she was back in the small bed of her childhood, back in the small space of the little girl who was afraid.

The hats, properly perched on stands as in all women's dreams of an actress wardrobe, were never taken down. They required such audacity. They demanded that a role be played to its maximum perfection. So each time she had reached into the joyous hat exhibit, looked at the treasured hats, she took again the little skull cap, the unobtrusive page and choir-boy cap.

The moment when her small hand hesitated, lavishing even a caress over the arrogant feather, the challenged upward tilts, the regal velvets, the labyrinthian veils, the assertive gallant ribbons, the plumage and decorations of triumph, was it doubt which reached for the tiny skull cap of the priest, choir boy and scholar?

Was it doubt which threw a suspicious glance over the shoes she had collected for their courage, shoes intended to walk the most entrancing and dangerous paths? Shoes of assurance and daring exploration, shoes for new situations, new steps, new places. All shined and polished for variety and change and adventure, and then each day rebuked, left like museum pieces on their shelves while she took the familiar and slightly worn ones that would not impose on her feet too large a role, too great an undertaking, shoes for the familiar route to the studio, to the people she knew well, to the places which held no surprises. . . .

Once when Stella was on the stage acting a love scene, which was taking place after a scene in a snowstorm, one of the flakes of artificial snow remained on the wing of her small and delicate nose. And then, during the exalted scene, the woman of warm snow whose voice and body seemed to melt into one's hands, the dream of osmosis, the dream of every lover, to find a substance that will confound with yours, dissolve, and yield and incorporate and become indissoluble—all during this scene there lay the snowflake catching the light and flashing signals of gently humorous inappropriateness and misplacement. The snowflake gave the scene an imperfection which touched the heart and brought all the feelings of the watchers to converge and rest upon that infinitely moving absurdity of the misplaced snowflake.

If Stella had known it she would have been crushed. The lightest of her defects, weighing no more than a snowflake, which touched the human heart as only fallibility can touch it, aroused Stella's self-condemnation and weighed down upon her soul with the oppressive weight of all perfectionism.

At times the woman on the screen and the woman she was every day encountered and fused together. And those were the moments when the impetus took its flight in full opulence and reached plenitude. They were so rare that she considered them peaks inaccessible to daily living, impossible to attain continuously.

But what killed them was not the altitude, the rarefied intensity of them. What killed them for her was that they remained unanswerable. It was a moment human beings did not feel together or in rhythm. It was a moment to be felt alone. It was the solitude that was unbearable.

Whenever she moved forward she fell into an abysm.

She remembered a day spent in full freedom by the sea with Bruno. He had fallen asleep late and she had slipped away for a swim. All through the swimming she had the impression of swimming into an ocean of feeling—because of Bruno she would no longer move separately from this great moving body of feeling undulating with her which made of her emotions an illimitable symphonic joy. She had the marvellous sensation of being a part of a vaster world and moving with it because of moving in rhythm with another being.

The joy of this was so intense that when she saw him approaching she ran towards him wildly, joyously. Coming near him like a ballet dancer she took a leap towards him, and he, frightened by her vehemence, and fearing that she would crash against him, instinctively became absolutely rigid, and she felt herself embracing a statue. Without hurt to her body, but with immeasurable hurt to her feelings.

Bruno had never seen her on the screen. He had seen her for the first time at a pompous reception where she moved among the other women like a dancer among pedestrians and distinguished herself by her mobility, by her voice which trembled and wavered, by her little nose which wrinkled when she smiled, her lips which shivered, the foreign accent which gave a hesitancy to her phrases as if she were about to make a portentous revelation, and by her hands which vibrated in the air.

He saw her in reality, yet he did not see Stella but the dream of Stella. He loved instantly a woman without fear, without doubt, and his nature, which had never taken flight, could now do so with her. He saw her in flight. He did not sense that a nature such as hers could be paralyzed, frozen with fear, could retreat, could regress, negate, and then in extreme fear, could also turn about and destroy.

For Stella this love had been born under the zodiacal sign of doubt. For Bruno, under the sign of faith.

In a setting of opulence, a setting of such elegance that it had required the wearing of one of the museum hats, the one with the regal feather, from two opposite worlds they came: Stella consumed with a hunger for love, and Bruno by the emptiness of his life.

As Stella appeared among the women, what struck Bruno was that he was seeing for the first time an animated woman. He felt caught in her current, carried. Her rhythm was contagious. He felt instantaneous obedience to her movement.

At the same time he felt wounded. Her eyes had pierced some region of his being no eyes had ever touched before. The vulnerable Bruno was captured, his moods and feelings henceforth determined, woven into hers. From the first moment they looked at each other it was determined that all she said would hurt him but that she could instantly heal him by moving one inch nearer to him. Then the hurt was instantly healed by the odor of her hair or the light touch of her hand on him.

An acute sense of distance was immediately established, such as Bruno had never known before to exist between men and women. A slight contradiction (and she loved contradiction) separated him from her and he suffered. And this suffering could only be abated by her presence and would be renewed as soon as they separated.

Bruno was discovering that he was not complete or autonomous.

Nor did Stella promise him completeness, nearness. She had the changing quality of dream. She obeyed her own oscillations. What came into being between them was not a marriage but an interplay where nothing was ever fixed. No planetary tensions, chartered and mapped and measured.

Her movements were of absolute abandon, yieldingness, and then at the smallest sign of lethargy or neglect, complete withdrawal and he had to begin courtship anew. Every day she could be won again and lost again. And the reason for her flights and departures, her breaks from him, were obscure and mysterious to him.

One night when they had been separated for many days, she received a telegram that he would visit her for a whole night. For her this whole night was as long, as portentous, as deep as a whole existence. She dwelt on every detail of it, she improvised upon it, she constructed and imagined and lived in it completely for many days. This was to be their marriage.

Her eyes overflowed with expectancy as she met him. Then she noticed that he had come without a valise. She did not seek the cause. She was struck by this as a betrayal of their love. Her being closed with an anguish inexplicable to him (an anguish over the possibility of a break, a separation, made her consider every small break, every small separation like a premonition of an ultimate one).

He spent his time in a struggle to reassure her, to reconquer her, to renew her faith, and she in resisting. She considered the demands of reality as something to be entirely crushed in favor of love, that obedience to reality meant a weakness in love.

Reality was the dragon that must be killed by the lover each time anew. And she was blind to her own crime against love, corroding it with the acid of her own doubt.

7

But a greater obstacle she had yet to encounter.

At the first meeting the dream of their encounter eclipsed the surrounding regions of their lives and isolated them together as inside a cocoon of silk and sensation. It gave them the illusion that each was the center of the other's existence.

No matter how exigent was the demand made upon Stella by her screen work, she always overthrew every obstacle in favor of love. She broke contracts easily, sailed at a moment's notice, and no pursuit of fame could interfere with the course of love. This willingness to sacrifice external achievements or success to love was typically feminine but she expected Bruno to behave in the same manner.

But he was a person who could only swim in the ocean of love if his moorings were maintained, the long established moorings of marriage and children. The stately house of permanency and continuity that was his home, built around his role in the world, built on peace and faith, with the smile of his wife which had become for him the smile of his mother—this edifice made out of the other components of his nature, his need for a haven, for children who were as his brothers had been, for a wife who was that which his mother had been. He could not throw over all these creations and possessions of his day for a night's dream, and Stella was that night's dream, all impermanency, vanishing and returning only with the night.

She, the homeless one, could not respect that which he respected. He, by respecting the established, felt free of guilt. He was paying his debt of honor and he was free, free to adore her, free to dream her. This did not appease her. Nor the simplicity with which he explained that he could not tear from its foundation the human home, with the children and the wife whom he protected. He could only love and live in peace if he fulfilled his promises to what he had created.

It was not that Stella wanted the wife's role or place. She knew deep down how unfitted she was for this role and to that side of his nature. It was merely that she could not share a love without the feeling that into this region of Bruno's being she did not care to enter, that there lay there a danger of death to their relationship. For her, any opening, any unconquered region contained the hidden enemy, the seed of death, the possible destroyer. Only absolute possession calmed her fear.

He was at peace with his conscience and therefore he feared no punishment for the joys she gave him. It was a condition of his nature. Because he had not destroyed or displaced, he felt he would not be destroyed or displaced and he could give his faith and joy to the dream. Her anguish and fears were inexplicable to him. For him there was no enemy ready to spring at her from the calm of his house.

If a telephone call or some emergency at home tore him away from her, for her it was abandon, and the end of love. If the time were shortened it signified a diminishing of love. If a choice were to be made she felt that he would choose his wife and children against her. None of these fatalistic signs were visible to him.

This hotel room was for him the symbol of the freedom of their love, the voyage, the exploration, the unknown, the restlessness that could be shared together, the surprises, the marvellously formless and bodiless and houseless freedom of this world created by two people in a hotel room. It was outside of the known, the familiar, and built only out of intensity, the present, with the great exalted beauty of the changing, the fluctuating, the dangerous and unmoored. . . .

Would she destroy this world created only on the fragrance of a voice, enhanced by intermittent disappearances? The privilege of travelling further into space and wonder because free of ballast? This marvellous world patterned only according to the irregularities of a dream, with its dark abysms in between, its change and flow and capriciousness?

Bruno clung desperately to the beauty, to the preciousness of this essence, pure because it was an essence. And for him even less threatened by death than his first love had been by the development of daily life. (For at a certain moment the face of his wife was no longer the face of a dream but became the face of his mother. At the same moment as the dream died, his home became the human and dreamless home of his boyhood, his children became the playmates of his adolescence.)

And Stella, when he explained this, knew the truth of it, yet she was the victim of a stronger demon, a demon of doubt blindly seeking visible proofs, the proofs of the love in reality which would most effectively destroy the dream. For passion usually has the instinctive wisdom to evade the test of human life together which is only possible to love. For Stella, because of her doubt, so desperately in need of reassurance, if he surrendered all to her it would mean that he was giving all his total love to their dream, whereas to him surrendering all meant giving Stella a lesser self (since passion was the love of the dreamed self and not the reality).

There was in this hotel room stronger proof of the strength of the dream, and Stella demanded proofs of its human reality and in so doing exposed its incompleteness, and hastened its end (Pandora's box).

Stella! he always cried out as he entered, enveloping her in the fervor of his voice.

Stella! he repeated, to express how she filled his being and overflowed within him, to fill the room with this name which filled him.

He had a way of saying it which was like crowning her the favorite. He made of each encounter such a rounded, complete experience, charged with the violence of a great hunger. Not having seen her upon awakening, not having helped to free her of the cocoon web of the night, not having shared her first contact with daylight, her first meal, the inception of her moods for that day, the first intentions and plans for action, he felt all the more impelled to catch her at the moment of the climax, to join her at the culmination. The lost, missed moments of life together, the lost, missed gestures, were thrown in desperation to feed the bonfire known only to foreshortened lives.

Because of all this that was lost around the love, the hotel room became the island, the poem and the paradise, because of all that was torn away, and sunk away.

The miracle of intensification.

Yet Stella asked, mutely, with every gasp of doubt and anguish: Let us live together (as if human life would give a certitude!). And he answered, mutely, with every act of faith: Let us dream together!

He arrived each day with new eyes. Undimmed by familiarity. New eyes for the woman he had not seen enough. New, intense, deeply seeing eyes, seeing her in her entirety each time like a new person.

As he did not see the process of her walking towards their island, dressing for it, resting for it, fighting off the inundation and de-

10

mands of other people to reach him, her presence seemed like an apparition, and he had to repossess her, because apparitions tend to disappear as they come, by routes unknown, into countries unknown.

There was between them this knowledge of the missing dimension and the need to recapture the lost terrain, to play the emotional detective for the lost fragments of the selves which had lived alone, as separate pieces, in a great effort to bring them all together into one again.

At his wrists the hair showed brilliant gold.

Hers dark and straight, and his curled, so that at times it seemed it was his hair which enveloped her, it was his desire which had the feminine sinuosities to espouse and cling, while hers was rigid.

It was he who surrounded and enveloped her, as his curled hair wound around the straightness of hers, and how sweet this had been in her distress and her chaos. She touched his wrists always in wonder, as if to ascertain his presence, because the joyousness of his coloring delighted her, because the smoothness of his movements was a preliminary to their accord and rhythms. Their movements toward each other were symphonic and preordained. Her divination of his moods and his of hers synchronized their movements like those of a dance. There were days when she felt small and weak, and he then increased his stature to receive and shelter her, and his arms and body seemed a fortress, and there were days when he was in need of her strength, days when their mouths transmitted all the fevers and hungers, days when frenzy called for an abandon of the whole body. Days when the caresses were a drug, or a symphony, or small secret duets and duels, or vast complex veilings which neither could entirely tear apart, and there were secrets, and resistances, and frenzies, and again dissolutions from which it seemed as if neither could ever return to the possession of his independence.

There was always this mingling of hairs, which later in the bath she would tenderly separate from hers, laying the tendrils before her like the signs of the calendar of their love, the unwitherable flowers of their caresses.

While he was there, melted by his eyes, his voice, sheltered in his tallness, encompassed by his attentiveness, she was joyous. But when

11

he was gone, and so entirely gone that she was forbidden to write him or telephone him, that she had in reality no way to reach him, touch him, call him back, then she became possessed again with this frenzy against barriers, against limitations, against forbidden regions. To have touched the point of fire in him was not enough. To be his secret dream, his secret passion. She must ravage and conquer the absolute, for the sake of love. Not knowing that she was at this moment the enemy of love, its executioner.

Once he stood about to depart and she asked him: can't you stay for the whole night? And he shook his head sadly, his blue eyes no longer joyous, but blurred. This firmness with which she thought he was defending the rights of his wife, and with which in reality he only defended the equilibrium of his scrupulous soul, appeared to her like a flaw in the love.

If Stella felt an obstacle placed before one of her wishes such as her wish that Bruno should stay the whole night with her when it was utterly impossible for him to do so, this obstacle, no matter of what nature, became the symbol of a battle she must win or else consider herself destroyed.

She did not pause to ask herself the reasons for the refusal, or to consider the validity of these reasons, the claims to which others may have had a right. The refusal represented for her the failure to obtain a proof of love. The removal of this obstacle became a matter of life and death, because for her it balanced success or failure, abandon or treachery, triumph or power.

The small refusal, based on an altogether separate reason, unrelated to Stella, became the very symbol of her inner sense of frustration, and the effort to overcome it the very symbol of her salvation.

If she could bend the will and decision of Bruno, it meant that Bruno loved her. If not, it meant Bruno did not love her. The test was as devoid of real meaning as the tearing of leaves on a flower done by superstitious lovers who place their destiny in the mathematics of coincidence or accident.

And Stella, regardless of the cause, became suddenly blind to the feelings of everyone else as only sick people can become blind. She became completely isolated in this purely personal drama of a refusal she could not accept and could not see in any other light but that of a personal offense to her. A love that could not overcome all obstacles (as in the myths and legends of romantic ages) was not a love at all.

(This small favor she demanded took on the proportions of the ancient holocausts demanded by the mystics as proofs of devotion.)

She had reached the exaggeration, known to the emotionally unstable, of considering every small act as an absolute proof of love or hatred, and demanding of the faithful an absolute surrender. In every small act of yielding Stella accumulated defenses against the inundating flood of doubts. The doubt devoured her faster than she could gather external proofs of reassurance, and so the love given her was not a free love but a love that must accumulate votive offerings like those made by the primitives to their jealous gods. There must be every day the renewal of candles, foods and precious gifts, incense and sacrifice and if necessary (and it was always necessary to the neurotic) the sacrifice of human life. Every human being who fell under her spell became not the lover, but the day and night nurse to this sickness, this unfillable longing, this ravenous devourer of human happiness.

You won't stay all night?

The muted, inarticulate despair these few words contained. The unheard, unnoticed, unregistered cry of loneliness which arises from human beings. And not a loneliness which could be appeased with one night, or with a thousand nights, or with a lifetime, or with a marriage. A loneliness that human beings could not fill. For it came from her separation from human beings. She felt her separation from human beings and believed the lover alone could destroy it.

The doubt and fear which accompanied this question made her stand apart like some unbending god of ancient rituals watching for this accumulation of proofs, the faithful offering food, blood and their very lives. And still the doubt was there for these were but external proofs and they proved nothing. They could not give her back her faith.

The word penetrated Stella's being as if someone had uttered for the first time the name of her enemy, until then unknown to her.

Doubt. She turned this word in the palm of her dreaming hands, like some tiny hieroglyph with meaning on four sides.

From some little tunnel of obscure sensations there came almost imperceptible signs of agitation.

13

She packed hurriedly, crushing the hat with the feather, breaking his presents.

Driving fast in her very large, too large, her movie star car, driving fast, too fast away from pain, the water obscured her vision of the road and she set the wipers in motion. But it was not rain that clouded the windows.

In her movie star apartment there was a small turning stairway like that of a lighthouse leading to her bedroom, which was watched by a tall window of square glass bricks. These shone like a quartz cave at night. It was the prism which threw her vision back into seclusion again, into the wall of the self.

It was the window of the solitary cell of the neurotic.

One night when Bruno had written her that he would telephone her that night (he had been banished once again, and once again had tried to reconquer her) because he sensed that his voice might accomplish what his note failed to do, at the moment when she knew he would telephone, she installed a long concerto on the phonograph and climbed the little stairway and sat on the step.

No sooner did the concerto begin to spin than the telephone rang imperatively.

Stella allowed the music to produce its counter-witchcraft. Against the mechanical demand of the telephone, the music spiralled upward like a mystical skyscraper, and triumphed. The telephone was silenced.

But this was only the first bout. She climbed another step of the stairway and sat under the quartz window, wondering if the music would help her ascension away from the warmth of Bruno's voice.

In the music there was a parallel to the conflict which disturbed her. Within the concerto too the feminine and the masculine elements were interacting. The trombone, with its assertions, and the flute, with its sinuosities. In this transparent battle the trombone, in Stella's ears and perhaps because of her mood, had a tone of defiance which was almost grotesque. In her present mood the masculine instrument would appear as a caricature!

And as for the flute, it was so easily victimized and overpowered. But it triumphed ultimately because it left an echo. Long after the

14

trombone had had its say, the flute continued its mischievous, insistent tremolos.

The telephone rang again. Stella moved a step farther up the stairs. She needed the stairs, the window, the concerto, to help her reach an inaccessible region where the phone might ring as any mechanical instrument, without reverberating in her being. If the ringing of the telephone had caused the smallest tremor through her nerves (as the voice of Bruno did) she was lost. Fortunate for her that the trombone was a caricature of masculinity, that it was an inflated trombone, drowning the sound of the telephone. So she smiled one of her eerie smiles, pixen and vixen too, at the masculine pretensions. Fortunate for her that the flute persisted in its delicate undulations, and that not once in the concerto did they marry but played in constant opposition to each other throughout.

The telephone rang again, with a dead, mechanical persistence and no charm, while the music seemed to be pleading for a subtlety and emotional strength which Bruno was incapable of rivalling. The music alone was capable of climbing those stairways of detachment, of breaking like the waves of disturbed ocean at her feet, breaking there and foaming but without the power to suck her back into the life with Bruno and into the undertows of suffering.

She lay in the darkness of her white satin bedroom, the mirrors throwing aureoles of false moonlight, the rows of perfume bottles creating false suspended gardens.

The mattress, the blankets, the sheets had a lightness like her own. They were made of the invisible material which had once been pawned off on a gullible king. They were made of air, or else she had selected them out of familiar, weighty materials and then touched them with her aerial hands. (So many moments when her reality was questionable—the time she leaped out of her immense automobile, and there on the vast leather seat lay such a diminutive pocketbook as no woman could actually use, the pocketbook of a midget. Or the time she turned the wheel with two fingers. There is a lightness which belongs to other races, the race of ballet dancers.)

Whoever touched Stella was left with the tactile memory of down and bonelessness, as after touching the most delicate of Persian cats.

15

Now lying in the dark, neither the softness of the room nor its whiteness could exorcise the pain she felt.

Some word was trying to come to the surface of her being. Some word had sought all day to pierce through like an arrow the formless, inchoate mass of incidents of her life. The geological layers of her experience, the accumulated faces, scenes, words and dreams. One word was being churned to the surface of all this torment. It was as if she were going to name her greatest enemy. But she was struggling with the fear we have of naming that enemy. For what crystallized simultaneously with the name of the enemy was an emotion of helplessness against him! What good was naming it if one could not destroy it and free one's self? This feeling, stronger than the desire to see the face of the enemy, almost drowned the insistent word into oblivion again.

What Stella whispered in the dark with her foreign accent enhancing strongly, markedly the cruelty of the sound was:

ma   soch   ism

Soch! Och! It was the och which stood out, not ma or ism but the och! which was like some primitive exclamation of pain. Am, am I, am I, am I, am I, whispered Stella, am I a masochist?

She knew nothing about the word except its current meaning: "voluntary seeking of pain." She could go no further into her exploration of the confused pattern of her life and detect the origin of the suffering. She could not, alone, catch the inception of the pattern, and therefore gain power over this enemy. The night could not bring her one step nearer to freedom. . . .

A few hours later she watched on the screen the story of the Atlantis accompanied by the music of Stravinski.

First came a scene like a Paul Klee, wavering and humid, delicate and full of vibrations. The blue, the green, the violet were fused in tonalities which resembled her feeling, all fused together and so difficult to unravel. She responded with her answering blood rhythms, and with the same sense she always had of herself possessing a very small sea, something which received and moved responsively in rhythm. As if every tiny cell were not separated by membranes, as

16

if she were not made of separate nerves, sinews, blood vessels, but one total fluid component which could flow into others, divine their feelings, and flow back again into itself, a component which could be easily moved and penetrated by others like water, like the sea.

When she saw the Paul Klee scene on the screen she instantly dissolved. There was no more Stella, but a fluid component participating at the birth of the world. The paradise of water and softness.

But upon this scene came the most unexpected and terrifying explosion, the explosion of the earth being formed, broken, reformed and broken anew into its familiar shape.

This explosion Stella was familiar with and had expected. It reverberated in her with unexpected violence. As if she had already lived it.

Where had she experienced before this total annihilation of a blue, green and violet paradise, a paradise of welded cells in a perpetual flow and motion, that this should seem like the second one, and bring about such a painful, physical memory of disruption?

As the explosions came, once, twice, thrice, the peace was shattered and blackened, the colors vanished, the earth muddied the water, the annihilation seemed total.

The earth reformed itself. The water cleared. The colors returned. A continent was born above.

In Stella the echo touched a very old, forgotten region. Through layers and layers of time she gazed at an image made small by the distance: a small figure. It is her childhood, with its small scenery, small climate, small atmosphere. Stella was born during the war. But for the diminutive figure of the child the war between parents—all division and separation—was as great as the world war. The being, small and helpless, was torn asunder by the giant figures of mythical parents striving and dividing. Then it was nations striving and dividing. The sorrow was transferred, enlarged. But it was the same sorrow: it was the discovery of hatred, violence, hostility. It was the dark face of the world, which no childhood was ever prepared to receive. In the diminutive and fragile vessel of childhood lies the paradise that must be destroyed by explosions, so that the earth may be created anew. But the first impact of hatred and destruction upon the child is sometimes too great a burden on its innocence. The being is sundered as the earth is by earthquakes, as the soul cracks under violence and hatred. Paradise (the scene of Paul Klee) was from the first intended to be swallowed by the darkness.

As Stella felt the explosions, through the microscope of her emotions carried backwards, she saw the fragments of the dispersed and sundered being. Every little piece now with a separate life. Occasionally, like mercury, they fused, but they remained elusive and unstable. Corroding in the separateness.

Faith and love united her to human beings as a child. She was known to have walked the streets at the age of six inviting all the passersby to a party at her home. She hailed carriages and asked the driver to drive "to where there were many people."

The first explosion. The beginning of the world. The beginning of a pattern, the beginning of a form, a destiny, a character. Something which always eludes the scientists, the tabulators, the detectives. We catch a glimpse of it, like this, through the turmoil of the blood which remembers the seismographic shocks.

Stella could not remember what she saw in the mirror as a child. Perhaps a child never looks at the mirror. Perhaps a child, like a cat, is so much inside of itself it does not see itself in the mirror. She sees a child. The child does not remember what he looks like.

Later she remembered what she looked like. But when she looked at photographs of herself at one, two, three, four, five years, she did not recognize herself. The child is one. At one with himself. Never outside of himself.

She could remember what she did, but not the reflection of what she did. No reflections. Six years old. Seven years old. Eight years old. Eleven. No image. No reflection. But feeling.

In the mirror there never appeared a child. The first mirror had a frame of white wood. In it there was no Stella. A girl of fourteen portraying Joan of Arc, La Dame Aux Camélias, Peri Banu, Carlota, Electra.

No Stella, but a disguised actress multiplied into many personages. Was it in these games that she had lost her vision of her true self? Could she only win it again by acting? Was that why now she refused every role—every role that did not contain at least one aspect of herself? But because they contained only one aspect of herself they only emphasized the dismemberment. She would get hold of one aspect, and not of the rest. The rest remained unlived.

The first mirror in which the self appears is very large, inlaid in a brown wood wall. Next to it a window pours down so strong a light that the rest of the room is in complete darkness, and the image of the girl who approaches the mirror is brought into luminous relief. It is the first spotlight, actually, the first aureole of lighting, bringing her into relief, but in a state of humiliation. She is looking at her dress, a dress of shiny, worn, dark blue serge which has been fixed up for her out of an old one belonging to a cousin. It does not fit her. It is meager, it looks poor and shrunk. The girl looks at the blue dress with shame.

It is the day she has been told at school that she is gifted for acting. They had come purposely into the class to tell her. She who was always quiet and did not wish to be noticed, was told to come and speak to the Drama teacher before everyone, and to hear the compliment on her first performance. And the joy, the dazzling joy which first struck her was instantly killed by the awareness of the dress. She did not want to get up, to be noticed. She was ashamed of the meager dress, its worn, its orphan air.

She can only step out of this image, this dress, this humiliation by becoming someone else. She becomes Melisande, Sarah Bernhardt, Faust's Marguerite, La Dame Aux Camélias, Thais. She is decomposed before the mirror into a hundred personages, and recomposed into paleness, immobility and silence.

She will never wear again the shrunken worn serge cast-off dress, but she will often wear again this mood, this feeling of being misrepresented, misunderstood, of a false appearance, of an ugly disguise. She was called and made visible to all, out of her shyness and withdrawal, and what was made visible was a girl dressed like an orphan and not in the costume of wonder which befitted her.

She rejects all the plays. Because they cannot contain her. She wants to walk into her own self, truly presented, truly revealed. She wants to act only herself. She is no longer an actress willing to disguise herself. She is a woman who has lost herself and feels she can recover it by acting this self. But who knows her? What playwright knows her? Not the men who loved her. She cannot tell them. She is

19

lost herself. All that she says about herself is false. She is misleading and misled. No one will admit blindness.

No one who does not have a white cane, or a seeing eye dog will admit blindness. Yet there is no blindness or deafness as strong as that which takes place within the emotional self.

Seeing has to do with awareness, the clarity of the senses is linked to the spiritual vision, to understanding. One can look back upon a certain scene of life and see only a part of the truth. The characters of those we live with appear with entire aspects missing, like the missing arms or legs of unearthed statues. Later, a deeper insight, a deeper experience will add the missing aspects to the past scene, to the lost character only partially seen and felt. Still later another will appear. So that with time, and with time and awareness only, the scene and the person become complete, fully heard and fully seen.

Inside of the being there is a defective mirror, a mirror distorted by the fog of solitude, of shyness, by the climate inside of this particular being. It is a personal mirror, lodged in every subjective, interiorized form of life.

Stella received a letter from Laura, her father's second wife. "Come immediately. I am divorcing your father."

Her father was an actor. In Warsaw he had achieved fame and adulation. He had remained youthful and the lover of all women. Stella's mother, whose love for him had encompassed more than the man, permitted him great freedom. It was not his extravagant use of this freedom which had killed her feeling for him, but his inability to make her feel at the center of his life, feel that no matter what his peripheries she remained at the center. In exchange for her self-forgetfulness he had not been able to give anything, only to take. He had exploited the goodness, the largeness, the voluntary blindness. He had dipped into the immense reservoir of her love without returning to it an equal flow of tenderness, and so it had dried. The boundlessness of her love was to him merely an encouragement of his irresponsibility. He thought it could be used infinitely, not knowing that even an infinite love needed nourishment and fecundation; that no love was ever self-sustaining, self-propelling, self-renewing.

And then one day her love died. For twenty years she had nour-

20

ished it out of her own substance, and then it died. His selfishness withered it. And he was surprised. Immensely surprised, as if she had betrayed him.

She had left with Stella. And another woman had come, younger, a disciple of his, who had taken up the burden of being the lover alone. Stella knew the generosity of the second wife, the devotion. She knew how deeply her father must have used this reservoir to empty it. How deeply set his pattern of taking without giving. Again the woman's love was emptied, burnt out.

"He threatens to commit suicide," wrote Laura, "but I do not believe it." Stella did not believe it either. He loved himself too well.

Stella's father met her at the station. In his physical appearance there was clearly manifested the fact that he was not a man related to others but an island. In his impeccable dress there was a touch of finite contours. His clothes were of an insulating material. Whatever they were made of, they gave the impression of being different materials from other people's, that the well pressed lines were not intended to be disturbed by human hands. It was sterilized elegance conveying his uniqueness, and his perfectionism. If his clothes had not carried this water-repellent, feeling-repellent quality of perfection, his eyes would have accomplished this with their expression of the island. Distinctly, the person who moved toward him was an invader, the ship which entered this harbor was an enemy, the human being who approached him was violating the desire of islands to remain islands. His eyes were isolated. They created no warm bridges between them and other eyes. They flashed no signal of welcome, no light of response, and above all they remained as closed as a glass door.

He wanted Stella to plead with Laura. "Laura suspects me of having an affair with a singer. She has never minded before. And this time it happens not to be true. I dislike being . . . exiled unjustly. I cannot bear false accusations. Why does she mind now? I can't understand. Please go and tell her I will spend the rest of my life making her happy. Tell her I am heartbroken." (As he said these words he took out his silver cigarette case and noticing a small clouded spot on it he carefully polished it with his handkerchief.) "I've been unconscious. I didn't know she minded. Tell Laura I had nothing to do with this woman. She is too fat."

21

"But if you had," said Stella, "wouldn't it be better to be truthful this time? She is angry. She will hate a lie now more than anything. Why aren't you sincere with her? She may have proofs."

At the word proof his neat, alert head perked, cool, collected, cautious, and he said: "What proofs? She can't have proofs. I was careful. . . ."

He is still lying, thought Stella. He is incurable.

She visited Laura, who was small and childlike. She was like a child who had taken on a maternal role in a game, and found it beyond her strength. Yet she had played this role for ten years. Almost like a saint, the way she had closed her eyes to all his adventures, the way she had sought to preserve their life together. Her eyes always believing, diminishing the importance of his escapades, disregarding gossip, blaming the women more often than him.

Today as she received Stella, for whom she had always had a strong affection, these same believing eyes were changed. There is nothing clearer than the mark of a wound in believing eyes. It shows clear and sharp, the eyes are lacerated, they seem about to dissolve with pain. The soft faith was gone. And Stella knew instantly that her pleading was doomed.

"My father's unfaithfulness meant nothing. He always loved you above all others. He was light, but his deep love was for you. He was irresponsible, and you were too good to him, you never rebelled."

But Laura defended her attitude: "I am that kind of person. I have great faith, great indulgence, great love. For that reason if someone takes advantage of this I feel betrayed and I cannot forgive. I have warned him gently. I was not ill over his infidelities but over his indelicacies. I wanted to die. I hoped he would be less obvious, less insolent. But now it is irrevocable. When I added up all his selfish remarks, his reckless gestures, the expression of annoyance on his face when I was ill, his indifferences to my sadness, I cannot believe he ever loved me. He told me such impossible stories that he must have had a very poor idea of my judgment. Until now my love was strong enough to blind me . . . but now, understand me, Stella, I see everything. I remember words of his he uttered the very first day. The kind of unfaithfulness women can forgive is not the kind your father was guilty of. He was not unfaithful by his interest in other women, but he betrayed what we had together: he abandoned me spiritually and emotionally. He did not feel for me. Another thing I cannot forgive him. He was not a natural man, but he was posing as an ideal being. He covered acts which were completely selfish under a coat of altruism. He even embroidered so much on this role of ideal being that I had all the time the deep instinct that I was being cheated, that I was living with a man who was acting. This I can't forgive. Even today he continues to lie. I have definite proofs. They fell into my hands. I didn't want them. And then he was not content with having his mistress live near me, he still wanted me to invite her to my house, he even taunted me for not liking her, not fraternizing with her. Let him cry now. I have cried for ten years. I know he won't kill himself. He is acting. He loves himself too much. Let him now measure the strength of this love he destroyed. I feel nothing. Nothing. He has killed my love so completely I do not even suffer. I never saw a man who could kill a love so completely. I say a man! I often think he was a child, he was as irresponsible as a child. He was a child and I became a mother and that is why I forgave him everything. Only a mother forgives everything. The child, of course, doesn't know when he is hurting the mother. He does not know when she is tired, sick; he does nothing for her. He takes it for granted that she is willing to die for him. The child is passive, yielding, and accepts everything, giving nothing in return but affection. If the mother weeps he will throw his arms around her and then he will go out and do exactly what caused her to weep. The child never thinks of the mother except as the all-giver, the all-forgiving, the indefatigable love. So I let my husband be the child. . . . But he, Stella, he was not even tender like a child, he did not give me even the kind of love a child has for the mother. There was no tenderness in him!" And she wept. (He had not wept.)

As Stella watched her she knew the suffering had been too great and that Laura's love was absolutely broken.

When she returned to her father carrying the word "irrevocable" to him, her father exclaimed: "What happened to Laura? Such a meek, resigned, patient, angelical woman. A little girl, full of innocence and indulgence. And then this madness. . . ."

He did not ask himself, he had never asked himself, what he must

23

have done to destroy such resignation, such innocence, such indulgence. He said: "Let's look at our house for the last time."

Until now it had been their house. But in reality the house belonged to Laura and she asked her husband not to enter it again, to make a list of his belongings and she would have them sent to him.

They stood together before the house and looked up at the window of his room: "I will never see my room again. It's incredible. My books are still in there, my photographs, my clothes, my scrap books, and I . . ."

At the very moment they stood there a slight earthquake had been registered in Warsaw. At that very moment when her father's life was shaken by the earthquake of a woman's rebellion, when he was losing love, protection, faithfulness, luxury, faith. His whole life disrupted in a moment of feminine rebellion. Earth and the woman, and this sudden rebellion. On the insensitive instrument of his egoism no sign had been registered of this coming disruption.

As he stood there looking at his house for the last time the bowels of the earth shook. Laura was quietly weeping while his life cracked open and all the lovingly collected possessions fell into an abysm. The earth opened under his perpetually dancing feet, his waltzes of courtship, his contrapuntal love scenes.

In one instant it swallowed the colorful ballet of his lies, his pointed foot evasions, his vaporous escapes, the stage lights and halos with which he surrounded and disguised his conquests and appetites. Everything was destroyed in the tumult. The earth's anger at his lightness, his audacities, his leaps over reality, his escapes. His house cracked open and through the fissures fell his rare books, his collection of paintings, his press notices, the gifts from his admirers.

But before this happened the earth had given him so many warnings. How many times had he not seen the glances of pain in Laura's eyes, how many times had he overlooked her loneliness, how many times had he pretended not to hear the quiet weeping from her room, how many times had he failed in ordinary tenderness . . . before the revolt.

"And if I get sick," he said, walking away from his house, "who will take care of me? If only I could keep the maid Lucille. She was wonderful. There never was anyone like her. She was the only one who knew how to press my summer suits. With her all my problems would be solved. She was silent and never disturbed me and she never left the house. Now I don't know if I will be able to afford her. Because if I have her it will mean I will have to have two maids. Yes, two, because Lucille is not a good enough cook."

Sadly he walked down the street with Stella's arm under his. And then he added; "Now that I won't have the car any more, I will miss the Fête des Narcisses at Montreux, and I am sure I would have got the prize this year."

While he balanced himself on the tight rope of his delusions, Stella had no fear for him. He could see no connection between his behavior and Laura's rebellion. He could not see how the most trivial remarks and incidents could accumulate and form a web to trap him. He did not remember the trivial remark he made to the maid who was devotedly embroidering a night gown for Laura during one of her illnesses. He had stood on the threshold watching and then said with one of his characteristic pirouettes: "I know someone on whom this nightgown would look more beautiful. . . ." This had angered the loyalty of the maid and later influenced her to crystallize the proofs against him. Everyone around him had taken the side of the human being he overlooked because they could see so obviously the enormous disproportion between her behavior towards him and his towards her. The greater her love, almost, the greater had grown his irresponsibility and devaluation of this love.

What Stella feared was a moment of lucidity, when he might see that it was not the superficial aspect of his life which had destroyed its basic foundation, but his disregard of and undermining of the foundation.

For the moment he kept himself balanced on his tight-rope.

In fact he was intently busy placing himself back on a pedestal. He was now the victim of an unreasonable woman. Think of a woman who bears up with a man for ten years, and then when he is about to grow old, about to grow wise and sedentary, about to resign from his lover's career, then she revolts and leaves him alone. What absolute illogicality!

"For now," he said, "I am becoming a little tired of my love affairs. I do not have the same enthusiasms."

After a moment of walking in silence he added: "But I have you, Stella."

The three loves of his life. And Stella could not say what she felt "You killed my love too."

Yet at this very moment she remembered when it happened. She was then a little girl of twelve. Her father and mother were separated and lived in opposite sections of the city. Once a week Stella's mother allowed her to visit her father. Once a week she was plunged from an atmosphere of poverty and struggle to one of luxury and indolence. Such a violent contrast that it came with a shock of pain.

Once when she was calling on her father she saw Laura there for the first time. She heard Laura laugh. She saw her tiny figure submerged in furs and smelled her perfume. She could not see her as a woman. She seemed to her another little girl. A little girl dressed and hairdressed like a woman, but laughing, and believing and natural. She felt warmly towards her, did not remember that she was the one replacing her mother, that her mother would expect her to hate the intruder. Even to this child of twelve it was clear that it was Laura who needed the protection, that she was not the conqueror. That in the suave, charming, enchanting manners of her actor father there lurked many dangers for human beings, for the vulnerable ones especially. The same danger as had struck her mother and herself: danger of abandon and loneliness.

Laura too was looking at Stella with affection. Then she whispered to her father and Stella with her abnormally sensitive hearing caught the last words, "buy her stockings."

(From then on it was Laura who assumed all her father's sentimental obligations, it was Laura who sent gifts to his mother, to her later.)

The father and daughter went off together through the most beautiful shopping streets of Warsaw. She had become acutely aware of her mended stockings now that Laura had noticed them. Her father would be ashamed of walking with her. But he did not seem concerned. He was walking now with the famous grace that the stage had so much enhanced, a grace which made it appear that when he bowed, or kissed a hand, or spoke a compliment, he was doing it with his whole soul. It gave to his courtships such a romantic totality that a mere bow over a woman's hand took on the air of a ceremony in which he laid his life at her feet.

He entered a luxurious cane shop. He had the finest canes spread before him. He selected the most precious of all woods, and the most delicately carved. He asked Stella for her approval. He emptied his pocketbook, saying: "I can still take you home in a cab." And he took her home in a cab. With his new, burnished cane he pointed out Stella's drab house to the cabman. With a gesture of romantic devotion, as if he were laying a red carpet under her feet, he delivered her to her poverty, to the aggressions of creditors, to the anxieties, the humiliations, the corroding pain of everyday want.

Today she was not walking with her father in mended stockings. But she was riding in taxis like an ambassador between Laura and her father. Laura sent her father an intricate Venetian vase on an incredibly slender stem which could not be entrusted to the moving van. Stella was holding it in one hand, her muff in the other, and at her feet lay packages of old love letters. And her father sent her back in the same taxi with a locket, a ring, photographs, letters.

Stella attended the thousandth performance of a play called *The Orphan* in which her father starred.

"*The Orphan*," he said, "that suits me well now, that is how I feel, abandoned by Laura." And speaking of the orphan, he the orphan, the abandoned one, the victim for the first time, he wept. (But not over Laura's pain, or broken faith.)

In the middle of the performance, when he was sitting in an armchair and speaking, suddenly his arms fell, and he sat stiffly back. It was so swift, so brusque, that he looked like a broken marionette. No man could break this way, so sharply, so absolutely. People rushed on the stage. "It's a heart attack." said the doctor.

Stella accompanied him to his house. He lay rigid as in death.

She could not weep. For him, yes, for his sadness. Not for her father. All links were broken. But a man, yes, any man who suffered. The darling of women. White hair and elegance. Solitude. All the women around him and none near enough. Stella unable to move nearer, because none could move nearer to him. He barred the way with his self-love. His self-love isolated him. Self-love the watchman, barring all entrance, all communication. One could not console him. He was dying because with the end of luxury, protection, of his role, his life ends. He took all his sustenance from woman but he never knew it.

It was not Stella who killed him. She had not been the one to say: you killed my love.

Pity convulsed her, but she could do nothing. He was fulfilling his destiny. He had sought only his pleasure. He was dying alone on the stage of self-pity.

But when he was lying down on a bench in the dressing room, his collar for the first time carelessly open, the fat doctor listening to his heart (breaking with self-pity), so slender, so stylized, so meticulously chiselled, like an effigy, a burning pity choked her.

Someone whose every word she had hated, whose every act and thought she condemned, whose every mannerism was false, every gesture a role, yet because this figure lay on a couch dying of self-pity, lay with his eyes closed in a supreme comedian's act, Stella could love and pity again. Does the love of the father never die, even when it is buried a million times under stronger loves, even when she had looked at him without illusion? The figure, the slenderness of the body, the fineness of its form, still escaped from the dark tomb of buried love and was alive, because he had so artfully lain down like a victim, fainted before a thousand people, because he had been an actor until the end; as for Laura, and Stella's mother— no one had seen or heard them weep.

A fragile Stella, lying in her ivory satin bed, amongst mirrors.

Her eloquent body can speak out all the feelings in the language of the dance. Now her hands lie tired on her knees, tired and defeated.

Her dance is perpetually broken by the wounds of love.

In her white nightgown she does not look like an enchantress but like an orphan.

In her white nightgown she runs out of her room downstairs to spare the servants an added fatigue, she the exhausted one.

Her body and face so animated that they do not seem made of flesh, but like antennae, breath, nerve.

Delicate, she lies back like a tired child, but so knowing.

Bright, she speaks as she feels, always.

Unreal—her voice vanishes to a whisper, as if she herself were going to vanish and one must hold one's breath to hear her.

Oriental, she takes the pose of the Bali dancers. Her head always free from her body like the bird's head so free from its fragile stem.

The language of her hands. As they curve, leap, circle, trepidate, one fears they will always end clasped in a prayer that no one should hurt her.

No role could contain her intensity.

She gave off such a brilliance in acting it was unbearable. Too great an exaltation for the role, which breaks like too small a vessel. Too great a warmth. The role was dwarfed, was twisted and lost. When she begged for the roles which could contain this intensity they were denied her.

Off the stage she continued the same mischievous wrinkling of her little nose, the same enhanced eyes, the child's ease and grace and impulsiveness (in the most pompous restaurant of the city she reached out towards a passing silver tray carried by a pompous waiter and stole a fried potato).

The intensity made the incidents she portrayed seem inadequate and small. There was a glow from so deep a source of feeling that it drowned the mediocre personages of the Hollywood gallery.

She ate like a child, avidly, as if in fear that it would be taken away from her, forbidden her by some parent. Like the child, she had no coquetry. She was unconscious of her tangled hair and liked her face washed of make-up. If someone made love to her while she still carried the weight of the wax on her eyelashes, if someone made love to her artificially exaggerated eyelashes, she was offended, as if by a betrayal.

She was a child carrying a very old soul and burdened with it, and wishing to deposit it in some great and passionate role. In Joan of Arc, or Marie Bashkirtseff . . . or Rejane, or Eleonora Duse.

There are those who disguise themselves, like Stella's father, who disguised himself and acted what he was not. But Stella only wanted to transform and enlarge herself and wanted to act only what she felt she was, or could be. And Hollywood would not let her. Hollywood had its sizes and standards of characters. One could not transgress certain limited standard sizes.

Philip. When Stella first saw him she laughed at him. He was too handsome. She laughed: "Such a wonderful Don Juan plumage," she said, and turned away. The Don Juan plumage had never charmed her.

But the next morning she saw him walking before her, holding himself as in a state of euphoria. She was still mocking his magnificence. But as he passed her, with a free, large, lyrical walk, he smiled at his companion so brilliant a smile, so wild, so sensual that she felt a pang. It was the smile of joy, a joy unknown to her.

At the same time she took a deeper breath into her lungs, as if the air had changed, become free of suffocating fogs, noxious poisons.

He was at first impenetrable to her, because the climate of lightness was anew to her.

She glided on the wings of his smile and his humor.

When she left him she heard the wind through the leaves like the very breath of life and again she breathed the large free altitudes where anguish cannot reach to suffocate.

She followed with him the capricious outlines of pure desire, trusting his smile.

The pursuit of joy. She possessed his smile, his eyes, his assurance. There are beings who come to one to the tune of music. She always expected him to appear in a sleigh, to the tune of sleigh bells. As a child she had heard sleigh bells and thought: they have the sound of joy. When she opened his cigarette case she expected the tinkling, light, joyous music of music boxes.

The absence of pain must mean it was not love but an enchantment. He came bringing joy and when he left she felt it was to go to his mysterious source and fetch some more. She waited without impatience and without fear. He was replenishing his supply. And every object he came in contact with was charged with the music that causes gayety to flower.

The knowledge that he was coming held her in a suspense of pleasure, that of a high, perilous trapeze leap. The long intervals between their meetings, the absence of love, made it like some brilliant trapeze incident, spangled, accompanied by music. She could admire their deftness and accuracy in keeping themselves outside of the circle of pain. The little seed of anguish to which she was so susceptible could not germinate in this atmosphere.

She laughed when he confessed to her his Don Juan fatigues, the exigencies of the role women imposed upon him. "Women keep such strict accounts and compare notes to see if you are always at the same level!" A weary Don Juan resting his head upon her knees. As if he knew that for her, awake or asleep, he was always the magician of joy.

He bore no resemblance to any other person or moment of her life. She felt as if she had escaped from a fatal, repetitious pattern.

One evening Stella entered a restaurant alone and was seated at the side of Bruno. So much time had passed and she felt herself in another world, yet the sight of Bruno caused her pain. He was deeply disturbed.

They sat together and lingered over the dinner.

At midnight Stella was to meet Philip. At eleven-thirty when she began to gather her coat, Bruno said: "Let me see you home."

Thinking of the possibility of an encounter between him and Philip (at midnight Philip was coming to her place), she showed hesitation. This hesitation caused Bruno such acute pain that he began to tremble. At all cost, she felt, he must not know. . . . So she said quickly: "I'm not going home. I'm expected at some friends'. I forgot them when I saw you. But I promised to drop in."

"Can I take you there?"

She thought: if I mention friends he knows, he will come with me. She said: "Just put me in a taxi."

This reawakened his doubts. Again a look of pain crossed his face, and Stella was hurt by it, so she said hastily and spontaneously: "You can take me there. It's on East Eighty-ninth."

While he talked tenderly in the taxi, she thought desperately that she must find a house with two entrances, of which there are many on Fifth Avenue, but as she had never been on East Eighty-ninth Street, she wondered what she would find on the corner, perhaps a club, or a private house, or a Vanderbilt mansion.

31

From the taxi window she looked anxiously at the big, empty lot on the right and the private house on the left. Bruno's voice so vulnerable, her fear of hurting him. Time pressing, and Philip waiting for her before the door of her apartment. Then she signalled the driver to stop before an apartment house on the corner of Eighty-ninth Street and Madison Avenue.

Then she kissed Bruno lightly but was startled when he stepped out with her and dismissed the taxi. "I need a walk," he said.

First of all the front door was locked and she had to ring for the doorman whom she had not expected to see quite so soon. As she continued to walk into the hallway, he asked. "Who do you want to see? Where are you going?"

She could only say: "There is a door on Madison Avenue?" This aroused his suspicion and he answered roughly: "Why do you want to know? Who do you want to see?"

"Nobody," said Stella. "I just came in here because there was a man following me and annoying me. I thought I might walk through and slip out of the other entrance and get a cab and go home."

"That door is locked for the night. You can't go through there."

"Very well, then, I'll wait here for a while until that man leaves."

The doorman could see through the door the figure of Bruno walking back and forth. What had happened? Was he considering trying to find her? Did he believe she had no friends in this house and that he would catch her coming out again? Was he intuitively jealous and wondering if his intuition was right? Waiting. He waited there, smoking, walking in the snowy night. She was sitting in the red-carpeted hall, in a red plush chair, while the doorman paced up and down, and Bruno paced up and down before the house.

Thinking of Philip waiting for her, sitting there, heart beating and pounding, mind whirling.

She stood up and walked cautiously to the door and saw Bruno still walking in the cold.

Pain and laughter, pain out of the old love for Bruno, laughter from some inner, secret sense of playing with difficulties.

She said to the doorman: "That man is still there. Listen, I must get away somehow. You must do something for me."

Not too gallantly, he called the elevator boy. The elevator boy took her down the cellar, through a labyrinth of grey hallways.

32

Another elevator boy joined them. She told them about the man who followed her, adding details to the story.

Passing trunks, valises, piles of newspapers, and rows and rows of garbage cans, then bowing their heads, they passed through one more alleyway, up some stairs and unlocked the back door.

One of the boys went for a taxi. She thanked them, with the gaiety of a child in a game. They said it was a great pleasure and that New York was a hell of a place for a lady.

In the taxi she lay low on the seat so that Bruno could not see her as they passed Madison Avenue.

Philip was in a state of anxiety over her lateness.

She wanted to say: you are not the one who should be anxious! It is you I came back to! I struggled to get to you. But I'm here. And Bruno it is who is standing outside, waiting in the cold.

One day Philip asked her to wait for him in his apartment because his train had been delayed. (Before that he had always come to her.) For the first time he wanted to find her there, in his own home.

She had never entered his bedroom.

It was the first time she stepped out of the ambience he created for her by his words, stories, actions. The missing dimensions of Philip she knew must exist but he had known how to keep them invisible.

And now late at night, out of idleness, out of restlessness, fumbling very much like a blind person left for the first time to himself, she began to caress the objects he lived with, at first with a tenderness, because they were his, because she still expected them to emit a melody for her, to open up with playful surprises, to yield to her finger an immediate proof of love. But none of them emitted any sound resembling him . . . And slowly her fingers grew less caressing, grew awkward. Her fingers recognized objects made for or given by women. Her fingers recognized the hairpins of the wife, the powder box of the wife, the books with dedications by women, the photographs of women. The fingerprints on every object were women's fingerprints.

Then in the bedroom she stared at his dressing table. She stared at an immaculate and "familiar" set of silver toilet articles. It was not that Philip had a wife, and mistresses, and belonged to the public

33

which awakened her. It was the silver toilet set on the dressing table, a replica of the aristocratic one which had charmed her childhood. Equally polished, equally symmetrically arranged. She was certain that if she lifted the hair brush it would be fragrant. Of course, it was fragrant.

The silver toilet set of her father had reappeared. And then of course, it made the analogy more possible. Everything else was there too—the wife, and the public, and the mistresses.

Her father receiving applause and the flowers of all women's tribute, the flowers of their femininity with the fern garnishings of multicolored hair given prodigally to the stage figures—the illusion needed for desire already artificially prepared for those too lazy to prepare their own. (In the love we have for those who are not on the stage the illusion has to be created by the love. The people who fall in love with the performers are like those who fall in love with magicians; they are the ones who cannot create the illusion or magic with the love—the mise-en-scene, the producer, the music, the role, which surrounds the personage with all that desire requires.)

In this love Philip will receive bouquets from women, and Stella will find again the familiar pain her father had given her, which she didn't want.

Because they had touched the ring around the planet of love, the outer ring of desire, had taken graceful leaps across visitless weeks, she had believed these to be marvelous demonstrations of their agility to escape the prisons of deep love's pains.

There were days when she felt: the core of this drama of mine is that at an early age I lost the element of joy. (In childhood we glimpse paradise, its possibility, we exist in it.) At what moment was it lost and replaced by anguish? Could she remember?

Standing before the silver brushes, combs and boxes on Philip's dressing table she remembered that just as other people watch the sun and rain for barometers to their moods, she had run every day to watch these silver objects. When her father was in stormy periods and ready to leave the house, they were disarranged and clouded. When he was in full bloom of success, harmony and pleasure they were symmetrically placed, and highly polished. The initials shone with exquisite iridescence. And on days of great discord and tragedy they disappeared altogether and were placed in their niches in his va-

34

lise. So she consulted them like the barometers of her emotional climate.

When he left the house altogether it seemed as if none of the objects that remained possessed this power to gleam, to shed a brilliance. It was a transition from phosphorescence to continuous greyness.

It was when he left that her life changed color. Because he took only the pleasure, he also shed this pleasure around him. When she was thrust out of this effulgence and away from the gleam of beautiful objects, she was thrust into sadness.

How could joy have vanished with the father?

A person could walk away without carrying everything away with him. He might have left a little casket from which she could draw joy at will! He could have left the silver toilet set. But no, he took everything away with him because he took away the faith, her faith in love, and left her the prey of doubts and fears.

Human beings have a million little doorways of communication. When they feel threatened they close them, barricade themselves. Stella closed them all. Suffocation set in. Asphyxiation of the feelings.

She appeared in a new story on the screen. Her face was immobile like a mask. It was not Stella. It was the outer shell of Stella.

People sent her enormous bouquets of rare flowers. Continued to send them. She signed the receipts, she even signed notes of thanks. Flowers for the dead, she murmured. With only a little wire, and a round frame, they would do as well.

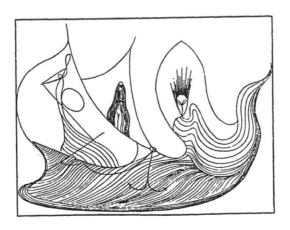

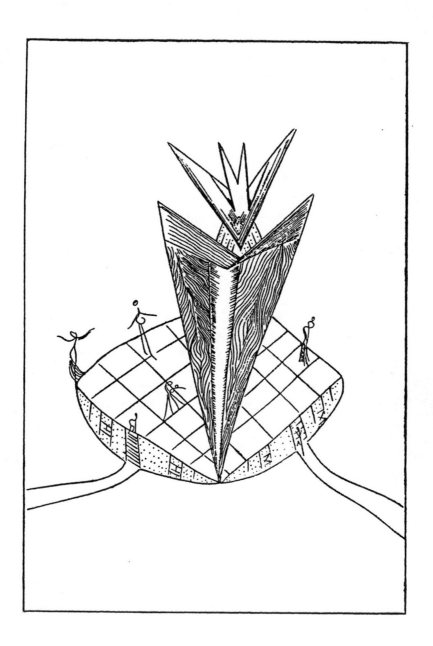

Winter of Artifice

SHE IS WAITING FOR HIM. She was waiting for him for twenty years. He is coming today.

This glass bowl with the glass fish and the glass ship—it has been the sea for her and the ship which carried her away from him after he had abandoned her. Why has she loved ships so deeply, why has she always wanted to sail away from this world? Why has she always dreamed of flight, of departure?

Today this past from which she has struggled so long to escape strikes her like a whip. But today she can bear the lash of it because he is coming and she knows that the circle of empty waiting will close.

How well she remembers their home near the sea, the villa which was in ruins. She was nine years old. She arrived there with her mother and two brothers. Her father was standing behind a window, watching. His face was pale, he did not seem glad to see them. She felt that he did not want them, that he did not want her. His anger seemed to be directed against all of them, but it touched her more acutely, as if it were directed entirely against her. They were not wanted, why she did not understand. Her mother said to him: It will be good for your daughter here. There was no smile on his face. He did not seem to notice that she was wasted by fever, that she was hungry for a smile.

There was never a smile on his face except when there were visitors, except when there was music and talk. When they were alone in the house there was always war: great explosions of anger, hatred, revolt. War. War at meals, war over their heads when her brothers and she were left in bed at night, war in the room under their feet when they were playing. War. War. . . .

In the closed study, or in the parlor, there was always a mysterious activity. Music, rehearsals, visitors, laughter. She saw her father in movement, always alert, tense, either passionately gay or passionately angry. When the door opened her father appeared, luminous, incandescent. A vital passage, even when he passed from one room to another. A gust of wind. A mystery. Not a reality like

37

her mother with her healthy red checks, her appetite, her frank natural laughter.

Never any serenity, never any time for caresses, for softness. Tension always. A life ripped by dissension. Even while they were playing the dark fury of their perpetual warring hung over them like threats and curses and recriminations. Never a moment of complete joy. Aware always of the battles that were about to explode.

One day there was a scene of such violence that she was terrified. An immense, irrational terror overwhelmed her. Her mother was goading her father to such anger that she thought he would kill her. Her father's face was blue-white. She began to scream. She screamed until they became alarmed. For a few days there was an interval of quiet. A truce. A pretense of peace.

The walls of her father's library were covered with books. Often she stole into the library and she read the books which she found there, books which she did not understand. Within her there was a well of secret thoughts which she could not express, which perhaps she might have formulated if someone had leaned over them with tenderness. The one person who might have aided her terrified her. Her father's eyes were always cold, critical, unbelieving. He would not believe the drawings she showed him were hers. He thought she had traced them. He did not believe that she had written the poems that were handed to him. He thought she had copied them. He flew into a rage because he could not find the books from which he had imagined she had copied her poems and drawings.

He doubted everything about her, even her illnesses. In the train once, going to Berlin where he was to give a concert, she had such an earache that she began to weep. If you don't stop crying and go to sleep, he said, I'll beat you. She stuffed her head under the pillow so that he would not hear her sobs. She sobbed all the way to Berlin. When they got there they discovered that she had an abscess in her ear.

Another time he was taken down with an attack of appendicitis. Her mother was tending him, fussing over him, running about anxiously. He lay there very pale in the big bed. She came from the street where she had been playing and told her mother that she was in pain. Immediately her father said: Don't pay any attention to her, she is just acting. She is just imitating me. But she did have an attack

38

of appendicitis. She had to be taken to the hospital and operated on. Her father, on the other hand, had recovered. He was in bed only three days.

Such cruelty! She asked herself,—was he really cruel, or was it mere selfishness? Was he just a big child who could not bear to have a rival, even in the person of his own daughter? She did not know. She was waiting for him now. She wanted to tell him everything. She wanted to hear what he had to say. She wanted to hear him say that he loved her. She did not know why she loved him so much. She could not believe that he meant to be so cruel. She loved him.

Because he was so critical, so severe, so suspicious of her, she became secretive and lying. She would never say what she really thought. She was afraid of him. She lied like an Arab. She lied to elude his stern glances, his cold, menacing blue eyes. She invented another world, a world of make-believe, of illusion, of games, of comedies. She tyrannized over her two brothers, she taught them games, she amused them, acted for them, enchanted them. She was a spitfire and they loved her. They never deserted her, even for a moment. They were simple, honest, frank. She complicated everything, even the games they played.

In Berlin, when she was five years old, she ran away. There was a seven-year-old boy waiting for her around the corner. His name was Heinrich.

She was a pale and sickly child. The doctor in Berlin had said: She must live in her native climate. Take her back. But there was no money for that. Her youngest brother had just been born. There was no money in the house, except for books and music, for a fur-lined coat, for the cologne water which her father had to sprinkle over his handkerchiefs, for the silk shirts which he demanded when he went on his concert tours.

At the villa near the sea she lay in bed and wept all night without knowing why. But there was a garden attached to the villa. A beautiful garden in which one could get lost. She sat by the big Gothic window studded with colored stones and looked out through a prismatic-colored stone in the center of the window; she sat there for hours at a stretch gazing upon this mysterious other world. Colors. Deformations. Trees that are ruby-colored. Orange skies. She felt that there were other worlds, that one might escape from this one which was so full of misery. She thought a great deal about this other world.

About her father there was an aureole of fragrance, of immaculateness, of elegance. His clothes were never wrinkled, he wore clean linen every day and the fur collar on his coat was wonderful to caress. Her mother was busy, bustling, maternal. Her mother was never elegant.

Since he often left them to go on concert tours they were so used to her father's departures that they barely ceased playing to embrace him. She remembered now the day he was leaving to go on tour. He was standing at the door, elegant, aristocratic. He looked the same as always. Suddenly, moved by an acute premonition, she threw herself on him and clung to him passionately. "Don't go, Father! Don't leave me!" she begged. She had to be torn away. She wept so violently that her father was startled. Even now she could feel again the effort her mother made to loosen her clutch. She could still see the hesitancy in her father's face. She begged and implored him to stay. She clung to him, desperately, her fingers knotted in his clothes. She remembered the effort he made to wrench himself loose and how he walked swiftly off without once looking back. She remembered too that her mother was surprised by her despair. She couldn't understand what had possessed her to behave as she did.

Since that day she had not seen her father. Twenty years have passed. He is coming today.

They entered New York harbor, her mother, her two brothers and she, in the midst of a violent thunderstorm. The Spaniards aboard the ship were terrified; some of them were kneeling in prayer. They had reason to be terrified,—the bow of the ship had been struck by lightning. She busied herself making a last-minute entry in her diary, which she had begun when they left Barcelona.

It was a monologue, or dialogue, dedicated to him, inspired by the superabundance of thoughts and feelings caused by the pain of leaving him. With the sea between them she felt that at least she might be able to reveal to him with absolute sincerity the great love she bore him, as well as her sadness and her yearning.

They arrived in New York with huge wicker baskets, a cage full of birds, a violin case and no money. She carried her diary in a basket. She was timid, withdrawn.

She caught only fleeting patches of this new reality surrounding her. At the pier there were aunts and cousins awaiting them. The Negro porters threw themselves on their belongings. She remembers vividly how she clung to her brother's violin case. She wanted everybody to know that she was an artist.

Entering the subway she observed immediately what a strange place New York was,—the staircases move up and down by themselves. And in the train hundreds of mouths chewing, masticating. Her little brother asked: "Are Americans ruminants?"

She was eleven years old. Her mother was absent most of the day searching for work. There were socks to darn and dishes to wash. She had to bathe and dress her brothers. She had to amuse them, aid them with their lessons. The days were full of bleak effort in which great sacrifices were demanded of all of them. Though she experienced a tremendous relief in helping her mother, in serving her faithfully, she felt nevertheless that the color and the fragrance had gone out of their life. When she heard music, laughter and talk in the room where her mother gave singing lessons, she was saddened by the feeling of something lost.

And so, little by little, she shut herself up within the walls of her diary. She held long conversations with herself, through the diary. She talked to her diary, addressed it by name, as if it were a living person, her other self perhaps. Looking out the window which gave on their ugly back yard she imagined that she was looking at parks, castles, golden grilles, and exotic flowers. Within the covers of the diary she created another world wherein she told the truth, in contrast to the multiple lies which she span when she was conversing with others, as for instance telling her playmates that she had traveled all around the world, describing to them the places which she had read about in her father's library.

The yearning for her father became a long, continuous plaint. Every page contained long pleas to him, invocations to God to reunite them. Hours and hours of suffocating moods, of dreams and reveries, of feverish restlessness, of morbid, somber memories and

41

longings. She could not bear to listen to music, especially the arias her mother sang; "Ever since the day," "Some day he'll come," etc. Her mother seemed to choose only the songs which reminded her of him.

She felt crippled, lost, transplanted, rebellious. She was alone a great deal. Her mother was healthy, exuberant, full of plans for the future. When she was moody her mother chided her. If she confessed to her mother, she laughed at her. Her mother seemed to doubt the sincerity of her feelings. She attributed her moods to her overdeveloped imagination, or else to her blood. When her mother was angry she shouted: *"Mauvaise graine, va!"* She was often angry now, but not with them. She was obliged to fight for them every day of her life. It required all her courage, all her buoyancy and optimism, to face the world. New York was hostile, cold, indifferent. They were immigrants, and they were made to feel it. Even on Christmas Eve her mother had to sing at the church in order to earn a few pennies.

The great crime, her mother made them feel, was their resemblance to their father. Each flare of temper, each tragic outburst was severely condemned. Even her paleness served to remind her mother of him. He too always looked pale and ready to die, but it was all nonsense, she said. Every day she added a little touch to the image they had of him. Her younger brother's rages, his wildness, his destructiveness, all this came from their father. Her imagination, her exaggerations, her fantasies, her lies, these, too, sprang from their father.

It was true. Everything sprang from him, even the lies which originated from the books she had read in his library. When she told the children at school that she had once traveled through Russia in a covered wagon it was not a lie either, because in her mind she had made this journey through snow-covered Russia time and time again. The cold of New York revived the memories of her father's books, of the journeys she had longed to take with him when he went away.

To face the cold of New York required superhuman efforts. Standing in the snow in Central Park, feeding the pigeons, she wanted to die. The dread of facing the snow and frost each morning paralyzed her. Their school was only around the corner, but she had not the courage to leave the house. Her mother had to ask the Negro janitor to drag her to school. "Po' thing," he would say, "you ought to live down South." He would lend her his woolen gloves and slap her back to get her warm.

Only in her diary could she reveal her true self, her true feelings. What she really desired was to be left alone with her diary and her dreams of her father. In solitude she was happy. Her head was seething with ideas. She described every phase of their life in detail, minute, childish details which seem ridiculous and absurd now, but which were intended to convey to her father the need that she felt for his presence. Though she detested New York, she painted a picture of it in glowing terms, hoping that it would entice him to come.

When, to amuse her brothers, she impersonated Marie Antoinette as she marched proudly to the guillotine, standing on a chariot of chairs with a lace cap, she wept real tears. She wept over the martyrdom of Marie Antoinette because she was aware of her own future sufferings. A million times her hair would turn white overnight and the crowd jeer at her. A million times she would lose her throne, her husband, her children, and her life. At eleven years of age she was searching in the lives of the great for analogies to the drama of her own life which she felt was destined to be shattered at every turn of the road. In acting the roles of other personages she felt that she was piecing together the fragments of her shattered life. Only in the fever of creation could she recreate her own lost life.

There was a passage in the diary wherein she wrote that she would like to relive her life in Spain. At that early age she was bemoaning the irreversibility of life.

Already she was aware of how the past dies. She re-examined what she had written about New York for her father because she felt that she had not done justice to it. She watched every minute of the day as she lived so that nothing would be lost. She regretted the minutes passing. She wept without knowing why, since she was young and had not yet known real suffering. But without being fully aware of it, she had already experienced her greatest sorrow, the irreparable loss of her father. She did not know it then, as indeed most of us never know when it is that we experience the full mea-

43

sure of joy or sorrow. But our feelings penetrate us like a poison of undetectable nature. We have sorrows of which we do not know the origin or name.

She remembered a night before Christmas when, in utter desperation she began to believe that her father was coming, that he would arrive Christmas Day. Even though that very day she had received a postcard from him and she knew that he was too far away for her hopes to be realized, still a sense of the miraculous impelled her to expect what was humanly impossible. She got down on her knees and she prayed to God to perform a miracle. She looked for her father all Christmas Day, and again on her birthday, a month later. Today he will come. Or tomorrow. Or the next day. Each disappointment was baffling and terrifying to her.

Today he is coming. She is sure of it. But how can she be sure? She is standing on the edge of a crater.

Her true God was her father. At communion it was her father she received, and not God. She closed her eyes and swallowed the white bread with blissful tremors. She embraced her father in holy communion. Her exaltation fused into a semblance of holiness. She aspired to saintliness in order to conceal the secret love which she guarded so jealously in her diary. The voluptuous tears at night when she prayed to God, the joy without name when she stood in his presence, the inexplicable bliss at communion, because then she talked with her father and she kissed him.

She worshiped him passionately but as she grew older the form of his image grew blurred. But she had not lost him. His image was buried deep in the most mysterious region of her being. On the surface there remained the image created by her mother—his egoism, his neglectfulness, his irresponsibility, his love of luxury. When for a time her immense yearning appeared to have exhausted itself, when it seemed that she had almost forgotten this man whom her mother described so bitterly, it was only the announcement of the fact that his image had become fluid; it ran in subterranean channels, through her blood. Consciously she was no longer aware of him; but in another way his existence was even stronger than before. Submerged, yet magically ineffaceable, he floated in her blood.

At thirteen she recorded in her diary that she wanted to marry a man who looked like the Count of Monte Cristo. Apart from the

44

mention of black eyes it was her father's portrait which she gave: "A man so strong . . . with very white teeth, a pale, mysterious face, . . . a grave walk, a distant smile. . . . I would like him to tell me all about his life, a very sad life, full of harrowing adventures. . . . I would like him to be proud and haughty . . . to play some instrument. . . ."

The image created by her mother, added to the blurred memories of a child, do not compose a being; yet in her haunting quest she fashioned an imagined individual she pursued relentlessly. The blue eyes of a boy in school, the talent of a young violinist, a pale face seen in the street—these fleeting aspects of the image that was buried deep in her blood moved her to tears. . . . To listen to music was unbearable. When her mother sang she exhausted herself in sobs.

In this record which she faithfully kept for twenty years she spoke of her diary as of her shadow, her double; "I say I will only marry my double." As far as she knew this double was the diary which was full of reflections, like a mirror, which could change shape and color and serve all kinds of imaginative substitutions. This diary she had intended to send to her father, which was to be a revelation of her love for him, became by an accident of fate, a secretive thing, another wall between herself and that world which it seemed forbidden her ever to enter.

She would have liked great love and tenderness, confidence, openness. Her father, she felt certain, would have rejected her—his standards were too severe. She wrote him once that she thought he had abandoned her because she was not an intelligent or pretty enough daughter. She was a perpetually offended being who fancied that she was not wanted. This fear of not being wanted weighed down on her like a perpetual icy condemnation.

Today, when he arrives, will she be able to lift her head? Will she be able to keep her head lifted, will she be able to stand the cold look in his eyes when she raises her eyes to his? Will her body not tremble with fear when she hears his voice? After twenty years she is still obsessed by the fear of him. But now she felt that it was in his power to absolve her of all fear. Perhaps it is he who will fear her. Perhaps he is coming to receive the judgment which she alone can mete out to him. Today the circle of empty waiting will be broken.

45

She is waiting for him to embrace her, to say that he loves her. She made a gòd of him and she was punished. Now when he comes she wants to make him a human father. She does not want to fear him any longer. She does not want to write another line in her diary. She wants him to smash this monument which she erected to him and accept her in her own right.

He is coming. She hears his steps.

She expected the man of the photographs, the young man of the photographs. She had not tried to imagine what the years had done to his face.

It was not any older, there were no wrinkles on it, but there was a mask over it. His face wore a mask. The skin did not match the skin of his wrists. It seemed made of earth and papier-mâché, not pure skin. There must have been a little space between it and the real face, a little partition through which the breeze could sing, and behind this mask another smile, another face, and skin like that of his wrists, white and vulnerable.

At the sight of her waiting on the doorstep he smiled, a feminine smile, and moved towards her with a neat, compact grace, ease, youthfulness. She felt unsettled. This man coming towards her did not seem at all like a father.

His first words were words of apology. After he had taken off his gloves, and verified by his watch that he was on time—it was very important to him to be on time—after he had kissed her and told her that she had become very beautiful, almost immediately it seemed to her that she was listening to an apology, an explanation of why he had left them. It was as if behind her there stood a judge, a tall judge he alone could see, and to this judge her father addressed a beautiful polished speech, a marvelous speech to which she listened with admiration, for the logic was so beautiful, the smooth change of phrases, the long and flawless story of her mother's imperfections, of all that he had suffered, the manner in which all the facts of their life were presented, all made a perfect and eloquent pleading, addressed to a judge she could not see and with whom she had nothing to do. He had not come out free of his past. Taking out a gold-tipped cigarette and with infinite care placing it in a holder which contained a filter

46

for the nicotine, he related the story she had heard from her mother, all with an accent of apology and deference.

She had no time to tell him that she understood that they had not been made to live together, that it was not a question of faults and defects, but of alchemy, that this alchemy had created war, that there was no one to blame or to judge. Already her father was launched on an apology of why he had stayed all winter in the south; he did not say that he enjoyed it, but that it had been absolutely essential to his health. It seemed to her as he talked that he was just as ashamed to have left them as he was of having spent the winter in the south when he should have been in Paris giving concerts.

She waited for him to lose sight of this judge standing behind her and then, plunging into the present, she said: "It's scandalous to have such a young father!"

"Do you know what I used to fear?" he said. "That you might come too late to see me laughing—too late for me to have the power to make you laugh. In June when I go south again you must come with me. They will take you for my mistress, that will be delightful."

She was standing against the mantelpiece. He was looking at her hands, admiring them. She leaned backwards, pushing the crystal bowl against the wall. It cracked and the water gushed forth as from a fountain, splashing all over the floor. The glass ship could no longer sail away—it was lying on its side, on the rock-crystal stones.

They stood looking at the broken bowl and at the water forming a pool on the floor.

"Perhaps I've arrived at my port at last," she said. "Perhaps I've come to the end of my wanderings. I have found you."

"We've both done a lot of wandering," he said. "I not only played the piano in every city of the world . . . sometimes when I look at the map, it seems to me that even the tiniest villages could be replaced by the names of women. Wouldn't it be funny if I had a map of women, of all the women I have known before you, of all the women I have had? Fortunately I am a musician, and my women remain incognito. When I think about them it comes out as a *do* or a *la*, and who could recognize them in a sonata? What husband would come and kill me for expressing my passion for his wife in terms of a quartet?"

47

When he was not smiling, his face was a Greek mask, his blue eyes enigmatic, the features sharp and willful.

He appeared cold and formal. She realized it was this mask which had terrorized her as a child. The softness came only in flashes swift as lightning, like breaks.

Unexpectedly, he broke when he smiled, the hardness broke and the softness which came was so feminine, so exposed, giving and seducing with the beauty of the teeth, exposing a dimple which he said was not a dimple at all, but a scar from the time he had slid down the banister.

As a child she had the obscure fear that this man could never be satisfied, by life, by human beings, by the world. Nothing but perfection would do. It was this sense of his exactingness which haunted her, an obscure awareness of his expectations which excited her to the great efforts she had made. But today she told herself that she had strained enough, that she wanted to rest, that she had waited a long time for it. She felt she did not want to appear before him until she was complete, and could satisfy him.

She wanted to enjoy. Her life had been a long strain, one long effort to surpass herself, to create, to perfect, a desperate and anxious flight upwards, always aiming higher, seeking greater difficulties, accumulating victories, loves, books, creations, always shedding yesterday's woman to pursue a new vision.

Today she wanted to enjoy. . . .

They were walking into a new world together, into a new planet, a world of transparency where all that happened to them since that day she clung to him so desperately was reduced to its essence, to a skeleton, to a silhouette. His vision and his talk were abstract; his rigorous selection acted like an intense searchlight which annihilated everything around them: the color of the room, the smell of *Tabac Blond,* the warmth of the log fire, the spring sunlight showing its pale face on the studio window, the flash of his gold ring flashing his coat of arms, the immaculateness of his shirt cuffs. Everything vanished around them, the walls, the rug under their feet, the satin rays of her dress, the orange rim of her sleeve, the orange reflections of the walls, the books leaning against each other, the soft backs of the French books yielding under the stiff-backed English books, the lightness and swiftness of his Spanish voice, his Spanish words bowing and smiling between the French.

She could only see the point he watched, the intense focusing upon the meaning of their lives, the clear outline of their patterns, and his questions: What are you today? What do you believe? What do you think? What do you read? What do you love? What is your music? What is your language? What is your climate? What hour of the day do you love best? What are your whims? Your extravagances? Your antipathies? Who are your enemies? Who is your god? Who is your demon? What haunts you? What frightens you? What gives you courage? Whom do you love? What do you remember? What image do you have of me? What have you been? Are we strangers, with twenty years between us? Does your blood obey me? Have I made you? Are you my daughter? Are you my father? Have we dreamed? Are we real? Is our life real? Is anything real? Are we here? Do I understand you?

"You are my daughter. We think the same. We laugh at the same things. You owe me nothing. You have created yourself alone, but I gave you the seed."

He was walking back and forth, the whole length of the studio, asking questions, and every answer she gave was the echo in his own soul. Echoes. Echoes. Echoes. Echoes. Blood echoes. Yes, yes to everything. Exactly. She knew it. That is what she hoped. The same: father and daughter. Unison. The same rhythm.

They were not talking. They were merely corroborating each other's theories. Their phrases interlocked.

She was a woman, she had to live in a world built by the man she loved, live by his system. In the world she made alone she was lonely. She, being a woman, had to live in a manmade world, could not impose her own, but here was her father's world, it fitted her. With him she could run through the world in seven-league boots. He thought and felt the same thing at the same time.

"Never knew anything but solitude," said her father. "I never knew a woman I could take into my world."

They did not speak of the harm they had done each other. The disease they carried in them they did not reveal. He did not know that the tragedy which had marked the first years of her life still colored it today. He did not know that the feeling of being abandoned was still as strong in her despite the fact that she knew it was not she who had been abandoned but her mother, that he had not really abandoned her but simply tried to save his own life. He did not know that this feeling was still so strong in her that anything which resembled abandon created a violent inner storm in her: a door closed on her too brusquely, a letter unanswered, a friend going away on a trip, the maid leaving to get married, the least mark of absent-mindedness, two people talking and forgetting to include her, or someone sending greetings to someone and forgetting her.

The smallest incident could arouse an anguish as great as that caused by death, and could reawaken the pain of separation as keenly as she had experienced it the day her father had gone away.

In an effort to combat this anguish she had crowded her world richly with friends, loves and creations. But beyond the moment of conquest there was again a desert. The joys given to her by friendships, loves, or a book just written, were endangered by the fear of loss. Just as some people are perpetually aware of death, she was perpetually aware of the pain of separation and the inevitability of it.

And beyond this, she also treated the world as if it were an ailing, abandoned child. She never put an end to a friendship of her own accord. She never abandoned anyone; she spent her life healing others of this fear wherever she saw it shadowed, pitying the whole world and giving it the illusion of faithfulness, durability, solidity. She was incapable of scolding, of pushing away, of cutting ties, of breaking relationships, of interrupting a correspondence.

Her father was telling her the story of the homely little governess he had made love to because otherwise she would never have known what love was. He took her out in his beautiful car and made her lie on the heather just as the sun was going down so he would not have to see too much of her face. He enjoyed her happiness at having an adventure, the only one she would ever have. When she came to his room in the hotel he covered the lamp with a handkerchief, and again he enjoyed her happiness, and taught her how to do her hair, how to rouge her lips and powder her face. The adventure made her almost beautiful.

He was talking about his escapades, skirting the periphery of his life, dwelling on his adventures. He did not dare to venture into the realm of deep love, for fear of discovering she had given her life to another. They wanted to give each other the illusion of having been faithful to each other always, and of being free to devote their whole life to each other, now that he had returned.

Love had not been mentioned yet. Yet it was love alone which obsessed them. Not music, nor writing, not painting, not decorating, not costuming, but love, the orchestration of love, its metamorphosis. She was living in a furnace of love, a blaze all around. Obsessional love, passionate love, sensual love, love in mystery, in darkness, in resistance, in contrast, love in fraternity, gratitude, imagination.

"I do think," he said, "that we should give up all this for the sake of each other. These women mean nothing to me. But the idea of devoting my whole life to you, of sacrificing adventures to something far more marvelous and deep, appeals so much to me. . . ."

"But mine is no adventure. . . .

"You should give him up. That isn't love at all. You know I've been your only great love. . . ."

She did not want to say: "Not my only great love," but he seemed to have guessed her thought because he turned his eyes completely away from her and added: "Remember, I am an old man, I haven't so many years left to enjoy you. . . ."

With this phrase, which was actually untrue because he was younger than most men of his age, he seemed to be asking her for her life, almost to be reaching out to take full possession of her life, just as he had taken her soul away with him when she was a child. It seemed to her that he wanted to take it away now again, when she was a full-blown woman. It seemed natural to him that she should have mourned his loss throughout her childhood. It was true that he was on the road to death, drawing nearer and nearer to it; it was also true that she loved him so much that perhaps a part of her might follow him and perish with him. Would she follow him from year to year, his withering, his vanishing? Was her love a separate thing, or a part of his life? Would she leave the earth with him today? He was asking her to leave the earth today, but this time she would not. This time she felt that she would fight against giving herself up wholly. She would not die a second time.

Having been so faithful to his image as she had been, having loved his image in other men, having been moved by the men who played the piano, the men who talked brilliantly, intellectuals, teachers, philosophers, doctors, every man with blue eyes, every man with an adventurous life, every Don Juan—was it not to give him her absolute love at the end? Why did she draw away, giving him the illusion he wanted but not the absolute?

In the south of France. Six silver-gray valises, the scent of *Tabac Blond,* the gleam of polished nails, the wave of immaculate hands. Her father leaped down from the train and already he was beginning a story.

"There was a woman on the train. She sent me a message. Would I have dinner with her? Knew all about me, had sung my songs in Norway. I was too tired, with this damnable lumbago coming on, and besides, I can't put my mind on women any longer. I can only think of my betrothed."

In the elevator he overtipped the boy, he asked for news of the Negro's wife who had been sick, he advised a medicine, he ordered an appointment with the hairdresser for the next day, he took stock of the weather predictions, he ordered special biscuits and a strict vegetarian diet. The fruit had to be washed with sterilized water. And was the flautist still in the neighborhood, the one who used to keep him awake?

In the room he would not let her help him unpack his bags. He was cursing his lumbago. He seemed to have a fear of intimacy, almost as if he had hidden a crime in his valises.

"This old carcass must be subjugated," he said.

He moved like a cat. Great softness. Yet when he wanted to he could show powerful muscles. He believed in concealing one's strength.

They walked out into the sun, he looking like a Spanish grandee. He could look straight into the sun, and the tenseness of his will when he said, for instance, "I want," made him rigid from head to foot, like silex.

As she watched him bending over so tenderly to pick up an insect from the road in order to lay it safely on a leaf, addressing it in a soft, whimsical tone preaching to it about its recklessness in thus crossing a road on which so many automobiles passed, she asked herself why it was that as a child she could only remember him as a cruel person. Why could she remember no tenderness or care on his part? Nothing but fits of anger and severity, of annoyance when they were noisy, of beatings, of a cold reserved face at meals.

As she watched him playing with the concierge's dog she wondered why she could not remember him ever sitting down to play with them; she wondered whether this conception she had of her father's cruelty was not entirely imaginary. She could not piece together his gentleness with animals and his hardness towards his children. He lived in his world like a scientist occupied with the phenomena of nature. The ways of insects aroused his curiosity; he liked to experiment, but the phenomena which the lives of his children offered, their secrets, their perplexities, had no interest for him, or rather, they disturbed him.

It was really a myopia of the soul.

The day after he arrived he was unable to move from his bed. A special medicine had to be found. Samba, the elevator man, was sent out to hunt for it. The bus driver was dispatched to get a special brand of English crackers. Paris had to be phoned to make sure the musical magazines were being forwarded. Telegrams and letters, telephone calls, Samba perspiring, the bus man covered with dust, postpone the hairdresser, order a special menu for dinner, telephone the doctor, fetch a newspaper, Samba perspiring, the elevator running up and down. . . .

There were no other guests in the hotel—the place seemed to be run for them. Their meals were brought to the room. Mosquito nettings were installed, the furniture was changed around, his linen sheets with large initials were placed on the bed, his silver hairbrushes on the dresser, the plumber ordered to subdue a noisy water pipe, the rusty shutters were oiled, the proprietor was informed that all hotel rooms should have double doors. Noise was his greatest enemy. His nerves, as vibrant as the strings of a violin, had endowed or cursed him with uncanny hearing. A fly in the room could prevent him from sleeping. He had to put cotton in his ears in order to dull his oversensitive hearing.

He began talking about his childhood, so vividly that she thought they were back in Spain. She could feel again the noonday heat, could hear the beaded curtains parting, footsteps on the tiled floors, the cool green shadows of shuttered rooms, women in white negligees, the smell of carnations, the holy water, the dried palms at the head of the bed, the pictures of the Virgin in lace and satin, wicker armchairs, the servants singing in the courtyard. . . .

He used to read under his bed, by the light of a candle so that his father would not find him out. He was given only one penny a week to spend. He had to make cigarettes out of straw. He was always hungry.

They laughed together.

He didn't have enough money for the Merry-go-Round. His mother used to sew at night so that he could afford to rent a bicycle the next day.

He looked out of the window from his bed and saw the birds sitting on the telegraph wires, one on each wire.

"Look," he said, "I'll sing you the melody they make sitting up there." And he sang it. "It's all in the key of humor."

"When I was a child I used to write stories in which I was always left an orphan and forced to face the world alone."

"Did you want to get rid of me?" asked her father.

"I don't think so. I think I only wanted to struggle with life alone. I was proud, and that also prevented me from coming to you until I felt ready. . . ."

"What happened in all those stories?"

"I met with gigantic difficulties and obstacles. I overcame them. I was handed a bigger portion of suffering than is usual. Without father or mother I fought the world, angry seas, hunger, monstrous stepparents, and there were mysteries, pursuits, tortures, all kinds of danger. . . ."

"Don't you think you are still seeking that?"

"Perhaps. Then there was another story, a story of a boat in a garden. Suddenly I was sailing down a river and I went round and round for twenty years without landing anywhere."

"Was that because you didn't have me?"

"I don't know. Perhaps I was waiting to become a woman. In all the fairy tales where the child is taken away she either returns when she is twenty, or the father returns to the daughter when she is twenty."

"He waits till she gets beyond the stage of having to have her nose blown. He waits for the interesting age."

Her father's jealousy began with the reading of her diary. He observed that after two years of obsessional yearning for him she had finally exhausted her suffering and obtained serenity. After serenity she had fallen in love with an Irish boy and then with a violinist. He was offended that she had not died completely, that she had not spent the rest of her life yearning for him. He did not understand that she had continued to love him better by living than by dying for him. She had loved him in life, lived for him and created for him. She had written the diary for him. She had loved him by falling in love at the age of eleven with the ship's captain who might have taken her back to Spain. She had loved him by taking his place at her mother's side and becoming logical and intellectual in imitation of him, not through any natural gifts for either. She had loved him by playing the father to her brothers, the husband to her mother, by giving courage, strength, by denying her feminine, emotional self. She had loved him in life creatively by writing about him.

It is true that she did not die altogether—she lived in creations. Nor did she wear black nor turn her back on men and life.

But when she became aware of his jealousy she began immediately to give him what he desired. Understanding his jealousy she began to relate the incidents of her life in a deprecatory manner, in a mocking tone, in such a way that he might feel she had not loved deeply anything or anyone but him. Understanding his desire to be exclusively loved, to be at the core of every life he touched, she could not bring herself to talk with fervor or admiration of all she loved or enjoyed. To be so aware of his feelings forced her into a role. She gave a color to her past which would be interpreted as: nothing that happened before you came was of any importance. . . .

The result was that nothing appeared in its true light and that she deformed her true self.

Today her father, looking at her, holding her book in his hand, studying her costumes, exploring her home, studying her ideas, says: "You are an Amazon. Until you came I felt that I was dying. Now I feel renewed and strengthened."

Her own picture of her life gave him the opportunity he loved of passing judgment, an ideal judgment upon the pattern of it.

But she was so happy to have found a father, a father with a strong will, a wisdom, an infallible judgment, that she forgot for the moment everything she knew, surrendered her own certainties. She forgot her own efforts, her own wisdom. It was so sweet to have a father, to believe that there could exist someone who was in life so many years ahead of her, and who looked back upon hers and her errors, who could guide and save her, give her strength. She relinquished her convictions just to hear him say: "In that case you were too believing," or: "That was a wasted piece of sacrifice. Why save junk? Let the failures die. It is something in them that make them failures."

To have a father, the seer, the god. She found it hard to look him in the eyes. She never looked at the food he put in his mouth. It seemed to her that vegetarianism was the right diet for a divine being. She had such a need to worship, to relinquish her power. It made her feel more the woman.

She thought again of his remark: "You are an Amazon. You are a force." She looked at herself in the mirror with surprise. Certainly not the *body* of an Amazon.

What was it her father saw? She was underweight, so light on her feet that a caricaturist had once pictured her as having floated up to the ceiling like a balloon and everybody trying to catch her with brooms and ladders. Not the woman in the mirror, then, but her words, her writing, her work. Strength in creation, in life, ideas. She had proved capable of building a world for herself. *Amazon!* Capable of every audacity in life, but vulnerable in love. . . .

She translated his remark to herself thus: Whenever anyone says *you are* they mean *I want you to be!* He wanted her to be an Amazon.

One breast cut off as in the myth, so as to be able to use the bow and arrow. The other breast far too tender, too vulnerable.

Why? Because an Amazon did not need a father. Nor a lover, nor a husband. An Amazon was a law and a world all to herself.

He was abdicating his father role. A woman-ruled world was no hardship to him, the artist, for in it he had a privileged place. He had all the sweetness of her one breast, together with all her strength. He could lie down on that breast and dream, for at his side was a woman who carried a bow and arrow to defend him. He, the writer, the musician, the sculptor, the painter, he could lie down and dream by the side of the Amazon who could give him nourishment and fight the world for him as well. . . .

She looked at him. He was her own height. He was a little bowed by fatigue and the thought of his own frailness. His nerves, his sensitiveness, his dependence on women. He looked slenderer and paler. He said: "I used to be afraid that my present wife might die. What would I do without a wife? I used to plan to die with her. But now I have you. I know you are strong."

Many men had said this to her before. She had not minded. Protection was a rhythm. They could exchange roles. But this phrase from a father was different . . . A father.

All through the world . . . looking for a father . . . looking naively for a father . . . falling in love with gray hairs . . . the symbol . . . every symbol of the father . . . all through the world . . . an orphan . . . in need of man the leader . . . to be made woman . . . and again to be asked . . . to be the mother . . . always the mother . . . always to draw the strength she had, but never to know where to rest, where to lay down her head and find new strength . . . always to draw it out of herself . . . from herself . . . strength . . . to pour out love . . . all through the world seeking a father . . . loving the father . . . awaiting the father . . . and finding the child.

His lumbago and the almost complete paralysis it brought about seemed to her like a stiffness in the joints of his soul, from acting and pretending. He had assumed so many roles, had disciplined himself to appear always gay, always immaculate, always shaved, always

57

faultless; he played at love so often, that it was as if he suffered from a cramp due to the false positions too long sustained. He could never relax. The lumbago was like the stiffness and brittleness of emotions which he had constantly directed. It was something like pain for him to move about easily in the realm of impulses. He was now as incapable of an impulse as his body was incapable of moving, incapable of abandoning himself to the great uneven flow of life with its necessary disorder and ugliness. Every gesture of meticulous care taken to eat without vulgarity, to wash his teeth, to disinfect his hands, to behave ideally, to sustain the illusion of perfection, was like a rusted hinge, for when a pattern and a goal, when an aesthetic order penetrates so deeply into the motions of life, it eats into its spontaneity like rust, and this mental orientation, this forcing of nature to follow a pattern, this constant defeat of nature and control of it, had become rust, the rust which had finally paralyzed his body. . . .

She wondered how far back she would have to trace the current of his life to find the moment at which he had thus become congealed into an attitude. At what moment had his will petrified his emotions? What shock, what incident had produced this mineralization such as took place under the earth, due to pressure?

When he talked about his childhood she could see a luminous child always dancing, always running, always alert, always responsive. His whole nature was on tiptoes with expectancy, hope and ardor. His nose sniffed the wind with high expectations of storms, tragedies, adventures, beauty. The eyes did not retreat under the brow, but were opened wide like a clairvoyant's.

She could not trace the beginning of his disease, this cancer of jealousy. Perhaps far back in his childhood, in his jealousy of his delicate sister who was preferred by his father, in his jealousy of the man who took his fiancée away from him, in the betrayal of his fiancée, in the immense shock of pain which sent him out of Spain.

Today if he read a clipping which did not give him the first place in the realm of music, he suffered. If a friend turned his admiration away. . . . If in a room he was not the center of attention. . . . Wherever there was a rival, he felt the fever and the poison of self-doubt, the fear of defeat. In all his relations with man and woman there had to be a battle and a triumph.

He began by telling her first of all that she owed him nothing; then he began to look for all that there was in her of himself.

What he noted in her diary were only the passages which revealed their sameness. She began naturally enough to think that he loved in her only what there was of himself, that beyond the realm of self-discovery, self-love, there was no curiosity.

Her father said: "Although I was prevented from training you, your blood obeyed me." As he said this his face shone with the luminosity of early portraits, this luminosity the one trait which had never faded from her memory. He glowed with a joyous Greek wisdom.

"We must look for light and clarity," he said, "because we are too easily unbalanced."

She was sitting at the foot of his bed.

"You've got such strong wings," he said. "One feels there are no walls to your life."

The mistral was blowing hot and dry. It had been blowing for ten days.

"Now I see that all these women I pursued are all in you, and you are my daughter, and I can't marry you! You are the synthesis of all the women I loved."

"Just to have found each other will make us stronger for life."

Samba the Negro came in with mail. When her father saw the letters addressed to her he said: "Am I to be jealous of your letters too?"

Between each two of these phrases there was a long silence. A great simplicity of tone. They looked at each other as if they were listening to music, not as if he were saying words. Inside both their heads, as they sat there, he leaning against a pillow and she against the foot of the bed, there was a concert going on. Two boxes filled with the resonances of an orchestra. A hundred instruments playing all at once. Two long spools of flute-threads interweaving between his past and hers, the strings of the violin constantly trembling like the strings inside their bodies, the nerves never still, the heavy poundings on the drum like the heavy pounding of sex, the throb of blood, the beat of desire which drowned all the vibrations, louder than any instrument, the harp singing god, god, and the angels, the purity in his brow, the clarity in his eyes, god, god, god, and the drums pounding desire at the temples. The orchestra all in one voice now, for an instant, in love, in love with the harp singing god and the violins shaking their hair and she passing the violin bow gently between her legs, drawing music out of her body, her body foaming, the harp singing god, the drum beating, the cello singing a dirge under the level of tears, through subterranean roads with notes twinkling right and left, notes like stairways to the harp singing god, god, god, and the faun through the flute mocking the notes grown black and penitent, the black notes ascending the dust route of the cello's tears, an earth tremor splitting the music in two fallen walls, walls of their faith, the cello weeping, and the violins trembling, the beat of sex breaking through the middle and splitting the white notes and black notes apart, and the piano's stairway of sounds rolling into the inferno of silence because far away, behind and beyond the violins comes the second voice of the orchestra, the dark voice out of the bellies of the instruments, underneath the notes being pressed by hot fingers, in opposition to these notes comes the song from the bellies of the instruments, out of the pollen they contain, out of the wind of passing fingers, the carpet of notes mourn with voices of black lace and dice on telegraph wires. His sadnesses locked into the cello, their dreams wrapped in dust inside of the piano box, this box on their heads cracking with resonances, the past singing, an orchestra splitting with fullness, lost loves, faces vanishing, jealousy twisting like a cancer, eating the flesh, the letter that never came, the kiss that was not exchanged, the harp singing god, god, god, who laughs on one side of his face, god was the man with a wide mouth who could have eaten her whole, singing inside the boxes of their heads. Friends, treacheries, ecstasies. The voices that carried them into serenity, the voices which made the drum beat in them, the bow of the violins passing between the legs, the curves of women's backs yielding, the baton of the orchestra leader, the second voice of locked instruments, the strings snapping, the dissonances, the hardness, the flute weeping

They danced because they were sad, they danced all through their life, and the golden top dancing inside them made the notes turn, the white and the black, the words they wanted to hear, the new faces of the world turning black and white, ascending and descending, up and down askew stairways from the bellies of the cello full of salted tears, the water rising slowly, a sea of forgetfulness.

Yesterday ringing through the bells and castanets, and today a single note all alone, like their fear of solitude, quarreling, the orchestra taking their whole being together and lifting them clear out of the earth where *pain is a long, smooth song that does not cut through the flesh, where love is one long smooth note like the wind at night, no blood-shedding knife to its touch of music from distance far beyond the orchestra which answered the harp, the flute, the cello, the violins, the echoes on the roof, the taste on the roof of their palates, music in the tongue, in the fingers when the fingers seek the flesh, the red pistil of desire in the fingers on the violin cords, their cries rising and falling, borne on the wings of the orchestra, hurt and wounded by its knowledge of her, for thus they cried and thus they laughed, like the bells and the castanets, thus they rolled from black to white stairways, and dreaming spirals of desire.*

Where is serenity? All their forces at work together, their fingers playing, their voices, their heads cracking with the fullness of sound, crescendo of exaltation and confusion, chaos, fullness, no time to gather all the notes together, sitting inside the spider web of their past, failures, defeats.

She writing a diary like a perpetual obsessional song, and he and she dancing with gold-tipped cigarettes, wrinkled clothes, vanity, and worship, faith and doubt, losing their blood slowly from too much love, love a wound in them, too many delicacies, too many thoughts around it, too many vibrations, fatigue, nervousness, the orchestra of their desire splitting with its many faces, sad songs, god songs, quest and hunger, idealization and cynicism, humor in the split-opened face of the trombone swelling with laughter. Walls falling under the pressure of wills, walls of the absolute falling with each part of them breathing music into instruments, their arms waving, their voices, their loves, hatreds, an orchestra of conflicts, a theme of disease, the song of pain, the song of strings that are never still, for after the orchestra is silent in their heads the echoes last, the concert is eternal, the solo is a delusion, the others wait behind one to accompany, to stifle, to silence, to drown. Music spilling out from the eyes in place of tears, music spilling from the throat in place of words, music falling from his fingertips in place of caresses, music exchanged between them instead of love, yearning on five lines, the five lines of their thoughts, their reveries, their emotions, their unknown self, their giant self, their shadow.

The key sitting ironically, half a question mark, like their knowledge of destiny. But she sat on five lines cursing the world for the shocks, loving the world because it has jaws, weeping at the absolute unreachable, the fifth line and the voice, saying always: have faith, even curses make music. Five lines running together with simultaneous song.

The poverty, the broken hairbrush, the Alice blue gown, twilight of sensations, MUSIQUE ANCIENNE, objects floating. One line saying all the time I believe in god, in a god, in a father who will lean over and understand all things. I need absolution! I believe in others' purity and I find myself never pure enough. I need absolution! Another line on which she was making colorful dresses, colorful houses, and dancing. Underneath ran the line of disease, doubt, life a danger, life a mockery with an evil mouth. Everything lived out simultaneously, the love, the impulse, the doubt of the love, the knowledge of the love's death, the love of life, the doubt, the ecstasy, the knowledge of its death germ, everything like an orchestra. Can we live in rhythm, my father? Can we feel in rhythm, my father? Can we think in rhythm, my father? Rhythm—rhythm—rhythm.

At midnight she walked away from his room, down the very long corridor, under the arches, with the lamps watching, throwing her shadow on the carpets, passing mute doors in the empty hotel, the train of her silk dress caressing the floor, the mistral hooting.

As she opened the door of her room the window closed violently—there was the sound of broken glass. Doors, silent closed doors of empty rooms, arches like those of a convent, like opera settings, and the mistral blowing. . . .

Over her bed the white mosquito netting hung like an ancient bridal canopy. . . .

The mystical bride of her father. . . .

It was she who told the first lie, with deep sadness because she did not have the courage to say to her father: "Our love should be great enough to be above jealousy. Spare me those lies which we tell the weaker ones."

Something in his eyes, a quicker beat of the eyelid, a wavering of the blue surface, the small quiver by which she had learned to detect jealousy in a face, prevented her from saying this. Truth was impossible.

At the same time there were moments when she experienced dark, strange pleasure at the thought of deceiving him. She knew how deceptive he was. She felt deep down that he was incapable of truth, that sooner or later he would lie to her, fail her. And she wanted to deceive him first, in a deeper way. It gave her joy to be so far ahead of her father who was almost a professional deceiver.

When she saw her father at the station a great misery overcame her. She sat inert, remembering each word he had said, each sensation.

It seemed to her that she had not loved him enough, that he had come upon her like a great mystery, that again there was a confusion in her between god and father. His severity, luminousness, his music, seemed again to her not human elements. She had pretended to love him humanly.

Sitting in the train, shaken by the motion, the feeling of the ever-growing distance between them, suffocating with a cold mood, she recognized the signs of an inhuman love. By certain signs she recognized all her pretenses. Every time she had pretended to feel more than she felt, she experienced this sickness of heart, this cramp and tenseness of her body. By this sign she recognized her insincerities. At the core nothing ever was false. Her feelings never deceived her. It was only her imagination which deceived her. Her imagination could give a color, a smell, a beauty to things, even a warmth which her body knew very well to be unreal.

In her head there could be a great deal of acting and many strange things could happen in there, but her emotions were sincere and they revolted, they prevented her from getting lost down the deep corridors of her inventions. Through them she knew. They were her eyes, her divining rod, they were her truth.

Today she recognized an inhuman love.

Lying back on the chaise longue with cotton over her eyes, wrapped in coral blankets, her feet on a pillow. Lying back with a feeling like that of convalescence. All weight and anguish lifted from the body and life like cotton over the eyelids.

She recognized a state which recurred often, in spite of light and sound, in spite of the streets she walked, her activities. A mood between sleep and dream, where she caught the corner of two streets—the street of dreams and the street of living—in the palm of her hand and looked at them simultaneously, as one looks at the lines of one's destiny.

There would come cotton over her eyes and long unbroken reveries, sharp, intense, and continuous. She began to see very clearly that what destroyed her in this silent drama with her father was that she was always trying to tell something that never happened, or rather, that everything that happened, the many incidents, the trip down south, all this produced a state like slumber and ether out of which she could only awake with great difficulty. It was a struggle with shadows, a story of not meeting the loved one but loving one's self in the other, of never seeing the loved one but of seeing reflections of his presence everywhere, in everyone; of never addressing the loved one except through a diary or a book written about him, because in reality there was no connection between them, there was no human being to connect with. No one had ever merged with her father, yet they had thought a fusion could be realized through the likeness between them but the likeness itself seemed to create greater separations and confusions. There was a likeness and no understanding, likeness and no nearness.

Now that the world was standing on its head and the figure of her father had become immense, like the figure of a myth, now that from thinking too much about him she had lost the sound of his voice, she wanted to open her eyes again and make sure that all this had not killed the light, the steadiness of the earth, the bloom of the flowers, and the warmth of her other loves. So she opened her eyes and she saw: the picture of her father's foot. One day down south, while they were driving, they stopped by the road and he took off his shoe which was causing him pain. As he pulled off his sock she saw the foot of a woman. It was delicate and perfectly made, sensitive and small. She felt as if he had stolen it from her: it was her foot she was looking at, her foot he was holding in his hand. She had the feeling that she knew this foot completely. It was her foot—the very same size and the very same color, the same blue veins showing and the same air of never having walked at all.

To this foot she could have said: "I know you." She recognized the lightness, the speed of it. "I know you, but if you are my foot I do not love you. I do not love my own foot."

A confusion of feet. She is not alone in the world. She has a double. He sits on the running board of the car and when he sits there she does not know where she is. She is standing there pitying his foot, and hating it, too, because of the confusion. If it were someone else's foot her love could flow out freely, all around, but here her love stands still inside of her, still with a kind of fright.

There is no distance for her to traverse; it chokes inside of her, like the coils of self-love, and she cannot feel any love for this sore foot because that love leaps back into her like a perpetually coiled snake, and she wants always to leap outside of herself. She wants to flow out, and here her love lies coiled inside and choking her, because her father is her double, her shadow, and she does not know which one is real. One of them must die so that the other may find the boundaries of himself. To leap out freely beyond the self, love must flow out and beyond this wall of confused identities. Now she is all confused in her boundaries. She doesn't know where her father begins, where she begins, where it is he ends, what is the difference between them.

The difference is this, she begins to see, that he wears gloves for gardening and so does she, but he is afraid of poverty, and she is not. Can she prove that? *Must* she prove that? Why? For herself. She must know wherein she is not like him. She must disentangle their two selves.

She walked out into the sun. She sat at a café. A man sent her a note by the garçon. She refused to read it. She would have liked to have seen the man. Perhaps she would have liked him. Some day she might like a very ordinary man, sitting at a café. It hadn't happened yet. Everything must be immense and deep. In this she was absolutely unlike her father who liked only the most superficial adventures.

Walking into the heart of a summer day, as into a ripe fruit. Looking down at her lacquered toenails, at the white dust on her sandals. Smelling the odor of bread in the bakery where she stopped for a roll. (This her father would not do.)

A cripple passed very close to her. Her face was burned, scarred, the color of iron. All traces of her features were lost, as on a leprous face. The whites of her eyes bloodshot, her pupils dilated and misty. In her flesh she saw the meat of an animal, the fat, the sinews, the blackening blood.

Her father had said once that she was ugly. He had said it because she was born full of bloom, dimpled, roseate, overflowing with

65

health and joy. But at the age of two she had almost died of fever. She lost the bloom all at once. She reappeared before him very pale and thin, and the aesthete in him said coolly: "How ugly you are!" This phrase she had never been able to forget. It had taken her a lifetime to disprove it to herself. A lifetime to efface it. It took the love of others, the worship of the painters, to save her from its effects.

His paternal role could be summed up in the one word: criticism. Never an élan of joy, of contentment, of approval. Always sad, exacting, critical, blue eyes.

Out of this came her love of ugliness, her effort to see beyond ugliness, always treating the flesh as a mask, as something which never possessed the same shape, color and features as thought. Out of this came her love of men's creations. All that a man said or thought *was* the face, the body; all that a man invented was his walk, his flavor, his coloring; all that a man wrote, painted, sang was his skin, his hair, his eyes. People were made of crystal for her. She could see right through their flesh, through and beyond the structure of their bones. Her eyes stripped them of their defects, their awkwardness, their stuttering. She overlooked the big ears, the frame too small, the hunched back, the wet hands, the webbed-foot walk . . . she forgave . . . she became clairvoyant. A new sense which had awakened in her uncovered the smell of their soul, the shadow cast by their sorrows, the glow of their desires. Beyond the words and the appearances she caught all that was left unsaid—the electric sparks of their courage, the expanse of their reveries, the lunar aspects of their moods, the animal breath of their yearning. She never saw the fragmented individual, never saw the grotesque quality or aspect, but always the complete self, the mask and the reality, the fulfillment and the intention, the core and the future. She saw always the actual and the potential man, the seed, the reverie, the intention as one. . . .

Now with her love of her father this concern with the truth lying beneath the surface and the appearance became an obsession because in him the mask was more complete. The chasm between his appearance, his words, his gestures, and his true self was deeper.

Through this mask of coldness which had terrified her as a child she was better able as a woman to detect the malady of his soul. His soul was sick. He was very sick deep down. He was dying inside;

his eyes could no longer see the warm, the near, the real. He seemed to have come from very far only to be leaving again immediately. He was always pretending to be there. His body alone was there, but his soul was absent: it always escaped through a hundred fissures, it was in flight always, towards the past, or towards tomorrow, anywhere but in the present.

They looked at each other across miles and miles of separation. Their eyes did not meet. His fear of emotion enwrapped him in glass. This glass shut out the warmth of life, its human odors. He had built a glass house around himself to shut out all suffering. He wanted life to filter through, to reach him distilled, sifted of crudities and shocks. The glass walls were a prism intended to eliminate the dangerous, and in this artificial elimination life itself was deformed. With the bad was lost the human warmth, the nearness.

There was no change in his love, but the mask was back again as soon as he returned to Paris. The whole pattern of his artificial life began again. He had stopped talking as he talked down south. He was conversing. It was the beginning of his salon life. There were always people around with whom he kept up a tone of lightness and humor. In the evenings she had to appear in his salon and talk with the tip of her tongue about everything that was far from her thoughts.

This was the winter of artifice.

In that salon, with its stained-glass windows, its highly polished floor, its dark couches rooted into the Arabian rugs, its soft lights and precious books, there was only a fashionable musician bowing.

Although in reality he had not abandoned her, she felt he had passed into a world she would not follow him into. She felt impelled to act out the scene of abandon from beginning to end. She wept at the isolation in which her father's superficiality left her. She told him she had surrendered all her friends and activities for him. She told him she could not live on the talks they had in his salon. Each phrase she uttered was almost automatic.

It was the scene she knew best, the one most familiar to her even though it became an utter lie. It was the same scene which had impressed her as a child, and out of which she had made a life pattern. As she talked with tears in her eyes, she pitied herself for having loved and trusted her father again, for having given herself to him, for having expected everything from him. At the same time she knew that this was not true. Her mind ran in two directions as she talked, and so did her feelings. She continued the habitual scene of pain: "I gave myself to you once, and you hurt me. I am glad I did not give myself to you again. Deep down I have no faith at all in you, as a human being."

The scene which she acted best and felt the best was that of abandon. She felt impelled to act it over and over again. She knew all the phrases. She was familiar with the emotions it aroused. It came so easily to her, even though she knew all the time that, except for the moment when he left them years ago, she had never really experienced abandon except by way of her imagination, except through her fear of it, through her misinterpretation of reality.

There seemed to be a memory deeper than the usual one, a memory in the tissues and cells of the body on which we tattoo certain scenes which give a shape to one's soul and life habits. It was in this way she remembered most vividly that as a child a man had tortured her; still she could not help feeling tortured or interpreting the world today as it had appeared to her then in the light of her misunderstanding of people's motives. She could not help telling her father that he was destroying her absolute love; yet she knew this was not true because it was not he who was her absolute love. But this statement was untrue only in time; that is, it was her father who had endangered her faith in the absolute, it was his behavior which she did not understand as a child which destroyed her faith in life and in love.

She knew she had deceived her father as to the extent of her love, but the thought in her mind was: what would I be feeling now if I had entrusted all my happiness to my father, if I had truly depended on him for joy and sustenance? I would be thoroughly despairing. This thought increased her sadness, and her face betrayed such anguish that her father was overwhelmed.

After this scene he continued his marionette life: a chain of fashionable concerts, of soirees, hairdressers, shirtmakers, newspaper clippings, telephone calls. . . .

She began to hate him for evaporating into frivolity, for disguising his soul with such puerilities.

She was filled with doubts. She saw him in a perpetually haunting shadow of something he was not. This man that he was not interfered with her actual knowledge. These encounters where love never reached an understanding, where all ended in frustration, this love which created nothing, this love strangled her life. As soon as he was away she began again to imagine him as he might be. She imagined him talking to her deeply, she imagined tenderness and understanding.

Imagined! Like a contagious disease withering her actual life, this imaginary meeting, imaginary talk, on which she spent all her inventiveness. As soon as he came all these expectations were destroyed. His talk was empty, marginal. His whole ingenuity was spent circling away from everything vital, in remaining on the surface by adroit descriptions of nothing; by a swift chain of puerilities, by long speeches about trivialities, by lengthy expansions of empty facts.

This ghost of her potential father tormented her like a hunger for something which she knew had been invented or created solely by herself, but which she feared might never take human shape. Where was the man she really loved? The windows he had opened in the south had been windows on the past. The present or the future seemed to terrify him. Nothing was essential but to retain avenues of escape.

This constant yearning for the man beyond the mask, this disregard of the mask, was also a disregard of the harm which the wearing of a mask inevitably produced. It was difficult for her to believe, as others did, that the mask tainted the blood, that the colors of the mask could run into the colors of nature and poison it. She could not believe that, like the women who had been painted in gold and died of the poison, the mask and the flesh could melt into each other and bring on infection.

Her love was based on faith in the purity of one's own nature. It made her oblivious of the deformities which could be produced in the soul by the wearing of a mask. It caused her to disregard the deterioration that might affect the real face, the habits which the mask could form if worn for a long time. She could not believe that if one pretended indifference long enough, the germ of indifference could finally grow, that the soul could be discolored by long pretense, that there could come a moment when the mask and the man melted into one another, that confusion between them corroded the vital core, destroyed the core. . . .

This deterioration in her father she could not yet believe. She expected a miracle to happen. So many times it had happened to her to see the hardness of a face fall, the curtain over the eyes draw away, the false voice change, and to be allowed to enter by her vision into the true self of others.

When she was sixteen she could feel his visitations. He would descend on her often when she was dancing and laughing. He came then like a blight, because when she felt his presence, she felt a curtain of criticism covering all things. She looked through his eyes then instead of her own. Her mother always said: laugh and dance, but her father in her was contemptuous. A strange intuition because she did not know then that her father could not dance.

Once she was dancing on the stage. She had just begun her first number. The Spanish music carried her away, whirled her into a state of delirium. She could feel the audience surrendering to her. She was dancing; carrying away their eyes, their senses, into her spinning and whirling.

Her eyes fell on the front row. She saw her father there. She saw his pale face half hidden in the audience. He was holding a program before his face in order not to be recognized. But she knew his hair, his brow, his eyes. It was her father. Her steps faltered, she lost her rhythm. Only for a moment. Then she swung around, stamping her feet, dancing wildly and never looking his way, until the end.

When she saw her father years later she asked him if he had been there. He answered that not only was he not there but that if he had had the power he would have prevented her from dancing because he did not want his daughter on the stage. Even from a distance she had felt his criticalness. Now she saw him as she had divined him, cold, formal, and conventional; and she was angry at the prison walls of his severity.

As soon as she left him everything began to sing again. Everybody she passed in the street seemed like a music box. She heard the street organ, the singing of the wheels rolling. Motion was music.

Her father was the musician, but in life he arrested music. Music melts all the separate parts of our bodies together. Every rusty fragment, every scattered piece could be melted into one rhythm. A note was a whole, and it was in motion, ascending or descending, swelling in fullness or thrown away, thrown out in the air, but always moving.

As soon as she left her father she heard music again. It was falling from the trees, pouring from throats, twinkling from the street lamps, sliding down the gutter. It was her faith in the world which danced again. It was the expectation of miracles which made every misery sound like part of a symphony.

Not separateness but oneness was music.

Father, let me walk alone into the music of my faith. When I am with you the world is still and silent.

You give the command for stillness, and life stops like a clock that has fallen. You draw geometric lines around liquid forms, and what you extract from the chaos is already crystallized.

As soon as I leave you everything fixed falls into waves, tides, is transformed into water and flows. I hear my heart beating again with disorder. I hear the music of my gestures, and my feet begin to run as music runs and leaps. Music does not climb stairways. Music runs and I run with it. Faith makes music come out of the trees, out of wood, out of ivory.

I could never dance around you, my father, I could never dance around you!

You held the conductor's baton, but no music could come from the orchestra because of your severity. As soon as you left my heart beat in great disorder. Everything melted into music, and I could dance through the streets singing, without an orchestra leader. I could dance and sing.

Walking down the Rue Saturne she heard the students of the Conservatoire playing the *"Sonate en Re Mineur"* of Bach. She also heard her mother's beautiful voice singing Schumann's *"J'ai pardonné."* . . . Strange how her mother, who had never forgiven her father, could sing that song more movingly than anything else she sang.

Walking down the Rue Saturne she was singing *"J'ai pardonné"*

71

under her breath and thinking at the same time how she hated this street because it was the one she always walked through on her way to her father's house. On winter evenings his luxurious home was heated like a hothouse, and she found him pale and tense, at work upon some trifling matter which he took very seriously. Or rehearsing, or else just coming down from his siesta.

This siesta he always took with religious care, as if the preservation of his life depended on it. At bottom he felt life to be a danger, a process not of growth but of deterioration. To love too deeply, he said, to talk too much, to laugh too much, was a wasting of one's energy. Life was an enemy to him, and every sign of its wear and tear gave him anxiety. He could not bear a crack in the ceiling, a bit of paint worn away, a stairway worn threadbare, a faded spot on the wallpaper. Since he never lived wholly in the moment a part of him was already preparing for the morrow.

When she saw her father coming out of his room after his siesta she always had the feeling that he was making artificial efforts to delay the process of growth, fruition, decay, disintegration, which is organic and inevitable.

He believed he was delaying death by preserving himself from life, when on the contrary, it was the fear of life and the efforts he made to avoid it which used up his strength. Living never wore one out as much as the effort not to live, she believed, and only if one lived fully and freely one also rested fully and deeply. Not trusting himself to life, not abandoning himself, he could not sink into deep sleep at night without fear of death. . . . She always left his house with a feeling of having come near to death because everything there was so clearly a fight against death.

She left the neatest, the most spotless street of Paris where the gardeners were occupied in clipping and trimming a few rare potted bushes in small, still front gardens; where butlers were occupied in polishing door knobs; where low cars rolled up silently and caught one by surprise; where stone lions watched fur-trimmed women kissing little dogs—everything that she had rejected—. . . .

The light was very strong on the newly painted street sign. And then she saw that the name of the street was being changed. Already it said: "Anciennement Rue Saturne . . . now changed to . . ."

Now changed. As she was changed and beginning to move away from the past. She wanted to change with the city, that all the houses of the past may be finally torn down, that the whole city of the past may disappear. That all she had seen, heard, experienced would cease to walk with her down streets with changed names, through the labyrinth of loss and change where all is forgotten. . . .

Each step along the Rue Saturne corresponded to a million steps she had taken away from her father. In the same city in which he lived a thousand steps took her to a different milieu, different ideas, different people.

Walking in the rain to pass before his house, looking up at the stained-glass window, thinking: I have at least eluded you. Where it is I have my deeper life, you do not know. The deepest part of my being you never penetrated. The woman who stands here is not your daughter. It is the woman who has escaped the stigmata of parental love.

To escape him she had run away to the end of the world. To be free of him she had run away to places where he never went. She had lost him, by living in the opposite direction from him. She sought out the failures because he didn't like those who stuttered, those who stumbled; she sought out the ugly because he turned his face away; she sought out the weak because they irritated him. She sought out chaos because he insisted on logic. She traveled to the other end of life, to the drab, the loose, the weak, the wine-stained, wine-soggy, in whom she was sure not to find the least trace of him. No trace of him anywhere along the Boulevard Clichy where the market people passed with their vegetable carts; no trace of him at two in the morning in the little café opposite La Trinite; no trace of him in the sordid neighborhood of the Boulevard Jean-Jaures; no trace of him in the *cinema du quartier,* in the Bal Musette, in the burlesque theatre. Never anyone who had heard of him. Never anyone who smelled like him. Never a voice like his.

It was her father who thrust her out into the black, soiled corners of the world. Everything she loved she turned her back on because it was also what he loved. Luxury with its serpentine of light, its masquerade costume of gaiety, everything that shined, glittered, threw off perfume, would have reminded her of him. To efface such a love took her years of walking greasy streets, of sleeping between soiled sheets, of traversing the unknown. She was happy only when she finally succeeded in losing him.

Her father and she were walking through the Bois. On his lips she could still see the traces of a mordant kiss.

"We met at Notre Dame," he was saying. "She began with the most vulgar cross-examination, reproaching me for not loving her. So I proceeded with a slow analysis of her, telling her she had fallen in love with me in the way women usually fall in love with an artist who is handsome and who plays with vehemence and elegance; telling her that it had been a literary and imaginary affair kindled by the reading of my books, that our affair had no substantial basis, what with meetings interrupted by intervals of two years. I told her that no love could survive such thin nourishment and that besides she was too pretty a woman to have remained two years without a lover, especially in view of the fact that she cordially detested her husband. She said she felt that my heart was not in it. I answered that I didn't know whether or not my heart was in it when we had only twenty minutes together in a taxi without curtains in an overlit city."

"Did you talk to her in that ironic tone?" she asked.

"It was even more cutting than that. I was annoyed that she had been able to give me only twenty minutes."

(He had forgotten that he had come to tell her that he did not love her. What most struck him and annoyed him was that she had only been able to escape her husband's surveillance for twenty minutes.)

"She was so hurt," he added, "that I didn't even kiss her."

As they walked along she again looked carefully at his lip. It was slightly red, with a deeper, bluish tone in one corner, where no doubt the dainty tooth of the countess had bitten most fiercely. But she did not say anything. She was reconstructing the scene more accurately in her own head. Probably the little countess had arrived at the steps of Notre Dame, looking very earnest, very exalted. Probably her father had been touched. She did not believe that her father had been annoyed by the countess's jealousy and worship, but that it had touched his vanity. He was disguising his pleasure under an air of indifference, so that his listener might take him for a cynical Don Juan, the despair of women.

He repeated a story which he had told her before, of how the countess had slashed her face in order to justify her tardiness to her husband. This story had always seemed highly improbable to her, because a woman in love is not likely to endanger her beauty. Any explanation would have been simpler than this farfetched tale of an automobile accident.

But why did he have this need of falsifying all that happened to him? She had long before asked him to cease creating this illusion of an exclusive love, to be truthful with her. She had offered to be his confidante. He had promised . . . and now he was inventing again.

When she arrived the next day he had not slept at all, thinking: I am going to lose you. And if I lose you I cannot live any more. You are everything to me. My life was empty before you came. My life is a failure and a tragedy anyway.

He looked deeply sad. His fingers were wandering over the keys, hesitantly. His eyes looked as if he had been walking through a desert.

"You make me realize," he said, "how empty my activity is. In not being able to make you happy I miss the most vital reason for living."

He was again the man she had known in the south. His tone rang true. But he could not let her be. If she preferred Dostoievsky to Anatole France he felt that his whole edifice of ideas was being attacked and endangered. He was offended if she did not smoke his cigarettes, if she did not go to all his concerts, if she did not admire all his friends.

And she—she wanted him to abandon his superficialities and vanities and deceptions. They could not accept each other.

Realizing more and more that she did not love him she felt a strange joy, as if she were witnessing a just punishment for his coldness as a father when she was a child. And this suffering, which in reality she made no effort to inflict since she kept her secret, gave her joy. It made her feel that she was balancing in herself all the injustice of life, that she was restoring in her own soul a kind of symmetry to the events of life.

It was the fulfillment of a spiritual symmetry. A sorrow here, a sorrow there. Abandon yesterday, adandon today. Betrayal today, betrayal tomorrow. Two equally poised columns. A deception here, a deception there, like twin colonnades: a love for today, a love for tomorrow; a punishment to him, a punishment to the other . . . and one for herself. . . . Mystical geometry. The arithmetic of the unconscious which impelled this balancing of events.

She felt like laughing whenever her father repeated that he was lucid, simple, logical. She knew that this order and precision were only apparent. He had chosen to live on the surface, and she to descend deeper and deeper. His fundamental desire was to escape pain, hers to face all of life. Instead of coming out of his shell to face the disintegration of their relationship he eluded the truth. He had not discovered as she had that by meeting the person she feared to meet, by reading the letter she feared to read, by giving life a chance to strike at her she had discovered that it struck less cruelly than her imagination. To imagine was far more terrible than reality, because it took place in a void, it was untestable. There were no hands with which to strike or defend oneself in that inner chamber of ghostly tortures. But in living the realization summoned energies, forces, courage, arms and legs to fight with so that war almost became a joy. To fight a real sorrow, a real loss, a real insult, a real disillusion, a real treachery was infinitely less difficult than to spend a night without sleep struggling with ghosts. The imagination is far better at inventing tortures than life because the imagination is a demon within us and it knows where to strike, where it hurts. It knows the vulnerable spot, and life does not, our friends and lovers do not, because seldom do they have the imagination equal to the task.

He told her that he had stayed awake all night wondering how he would bring himself to tell a singer that she had no voice at all.

"There was almost a drama here yesterday with Laura about that singer. I tried to dissuade her from falling in love with me by assuring her she was simply the victim of a mirage which surrounds every artist, that if she came close to me she would be disillusioned. So yesterday after the singing we talked for three quarters of an hour and when I told her I would not have an affair with her (at another period of my life I might have done it, for the game of it, but now I have other things to live for) she began to sob violently and the rimmel came off. When she had used up her handkerchief I was forced to lend her mine. Then she dropped her lipstick and I picked it up and wiped it with another of my handkerchiefs. After the first fits of tears she began to calmly make up her face, wiping off the rouge that had been messed up by the tears. When she left I threw the handkerchiefs into the laundry. The *femme de chambre* picked them up and left all the laundry just outside the door of my room while she was cleaning it. Laura passed by, saw them and immediately thought I had deceived her. I had to explain everything to her; I told her I had not told her about this woman because I did not want to seem to be boasting all the time about women pursuing me."

She did not mind his philandering, but she was eager for the truth. She knew that he was telling a lie, because when a woman weeps the rimmel comes off, but not the lipstick, and besides, all elegant women have acquired a technique of weeping which has no such fatal effect on the make-up. You wept just enough to fill the eyes with tears and no more. No overflow. The tears stay inside the cups of the eyes, the rimmel is preserved, and yet the sadness is sufficiently expressive. After a moment one can repeat the process with the same dexterity which enables the garçon to fill a liqueur glass exactly to the brim. One tear too much could bring about a catastrophe, but these only came uncontrolled in the case of a deep love.

She was smiling to herself at his naive lies. The truth probably was that he had wiped his own mouth after kissing the singer.

He was playing around now as before, but he hated to admit it to himself, and to her, because of the ideal image he carried in himself, the image of a man who could be so deeply disturbed and altered by the love of a long-lost daughter that his career as a Don Juan had come to an abrupt end.

This romantic gesture which he was unable to make attracted him so much that he had to pretend he was making it, just as she had often pretended to be taking a voyage by writing letters on the stationery of some famous ocean liner.

"I said to Laura: do you really think that if I wanted to deceive you I would do it in such an obvious and stupid way, right here in our own home where you might come in any moment?"

What her father was attempting was to create an ideal world for her in which Don Juan, for the sake of his daughter, renounced all women. But she could not be deceived by his inventions. She was too clairvoyant. That was the pity of it. She could not believe in that which she wanted others to believe in—in a world made as one wanted it, an ideal world. She no longer believed in an ideal world.

And her father, what did he want and need? The illusion, which she was fostering, of a daughter who had never loved any one but him? Or did he find it hard to believe her too? When she left him in the south, did he not doubt her reason for leaving him?

When she went about dreaming of satisfying the world's hunger for illusion did she know it was the most painful, the most insatiable hunger? Did she not know too that she suffered from doubt, and that although she was able to work miracles for others she had no faith that the fairy tale would ever work out for herself? Even the gifts she received were difficult for her to love, because she knew that they would soon be taken away from her, just as her father had been taken away from her when she loved him so passionately, just as every home she had as a child had been disrupted, sold, lost, just as every country she became attached to was soon changed for another country, just as all her childhood had been loss, change, instability.

When she entered his house which was all in brown, brown wood on the walls, brown rugs, brown furniture, she thought of Spengler writing about brown as the color of philosophy. His windows were not open on the street, he had no use for the street, and so he had made the windows of stained glass. He lived within the heart of his own home as Orientals live within their citadel. Out of reach of passers-by. The house might have been anywhere—in England, Holland, Germany, America. There was no stamp of nationality upon it, no air from the outside. It was the house of the self, the house of his thoughts. The wall of the self-created without connection with the crowd, or country or race.

He was still taking his siesta. She sat near the long range of files, the long, beautiful, neat rows of files, with names which set her dreaming: China, Science, Photography, Ancient Instruments, Egypt, Morocco, Cancer, Radio, Inventions, The Guitar, Spain. It required hours of work every day: newspapers and magazines had to be read and clippings cut out, dated, glued. He wove a veritable spider web about himself. No man was ever more completely installed in the realm of possessions.

He spent hours inventing new ways of filling his cigarette holder with an anti-nicotine filter. He bought drugs in wholesale quantities. His closets were filled with photographs, with supplies of writing paper and medicines sufficient to last for years. It was as if he feared to find himself suddenly empty handed. His house was a storehouse of supplies which revealed his way of living too far ahead of himself, a fight against the improvised, the unexpected. He had prepared a fortress against need, war and change.

In proportion to her father's capacity for becoming invisible, untouchable, unattainable, in proportion to his capacity for metamorphosis, he had made the most solid house, the strongest walls, the heaviest furniture, the most heavily loaded bookcases, the most completely filled and catalogued universe. Everything to testify to his presence, his duration, his signature to a contract to remain on earth, visible at moments through his possessions.

In her mind she saw him asleep upstairs, with his elbow under his chin, in the most uncomfortable position which he had trained himself to hold so as not to sleep with his mouth open because that was ugly. She saw him asleep without a pillow, because a pillow under the head caused wrinkles. She pictured the bottle of alcohol which her mother had laughingly said that he bottled himself in at night in order to keep young forever. . . .

He washed his hands continuously. He had a mania for washing and disinfecting himself. The fear of microbes played a very important part in his life. The fruit had to be washed with filtered water. His mouth must be disinfected. The silverware must be passed over an alcohol lamp like the doctor's instruments. He never ate the part of the bread which his fingers had touched.

Her father had never imagined that he may have been trying to cleanse and disinfect his soul of his lies, his callousness, his deceptions. For him the only danger came from the microbes which attacked the body. He had not studied the microbe of conscience which eats into the soul.

When she saw him washing his hands, while watching the soap foaming she could see him again arriving behind stage at a concert, with his fur-lined coat and white silk scarf, and being immediately surrounded by women. She was seven years old, dressed in a starched dress and white gloves, and sitting in the front row with her mother and brothers. She was trembling because her father had said severely: "And above all, don't make a cheap family show of your enthusiasm. Clap discreetly. Don't have people notice that the pianist's children are clapping away like noisy peasants." This enthusiasm which must be held in check was a great burden for a child's soul. She had never been able to curb a joy or sorrow: to restrain meant to kill, to bury. This cemetery of strangled emotions—was it this her father was trying to wash away? And the day she told him she was pregnant and he said: "Now you're worth less on the market as a woman" . . . was this being washed away? No insight into the feelings of others. Passing from hardness to sentimentality. No intermediate human feeling, but extreme poles of indifference and weakness which never made the human equation. Too hot or too cold, blood cold and heart weak, blood hot and heart cold.

While he was washing his hands with that expression she had seen on the faces of people in India thrust into the Ganges, of Egyptians plunged into the Nile, of Negroes dipped into the Mississippi, she saw the fruit being washed and mineral water poured into his glass. Sterilized water to wash away the microbes, but his soul unwashed, unwashable, yearning to be free of the microbe of conscience. . . . All the water running from the modern tap, running from this modern bathroom, all the rivers of Egypt, of India, of America . . . and he unwashed . . . washing his modern body, washing . . . washing . . . washing. . . . A drop of holy water with which to exorcise the guilt. Hands washed over and over again in the hope of a miracle, and no miracle comes from the taps of modern washstands, no holy water flows through leaden pipes, no holy water flows under the bridges of Paris because the man standing at the tap has no faith and no awareness of his soul: he believes he is merely washing the stain of microbes from his hands. . . .

She told her father she must leave on a trip. He said: "You are deserting me!"

He talked rapidly, breathlessly, and left very hurriedly. She wanted to stop him and ask him to give her back her soul. She hated him for the way he descended the stairs as if he had been cast out, wounded by jealousy.

She hated him because she could not remain detached, nor remain standing at the top of the stairs watching him depart. She felt herself going down with him, within him, because his pain and flight were so familiar to her. She descended with him, and lost herself, passed into him, became one with him like his shadow. She felt herself empty, and dissolving into his pain. She knew that when he reached the street he would hail a taxi, and feel relief at escaping from the person who had inflicted the wound. There was always the power of escape, and rebellion.

The organ grinder would play and the pain would gnaw deeper, bitterer. He would curse the lead-colored day which intensified the sorrow because they both were born inextricably woven into the moods of nature. He would curse his pain which distorted faces and events into one long, continuous nightmare.

She wanted to beg her father to say that he had not felt all this, and assure her that she had stayed at the top of the stairs, with separate, distinct feelings. But she was not there. She was walking with him, and sharing his feelings. She was trying to reach out to him and reassure him. But everything about him was fluttering like a bird that had flown into a room by mistake, flying recklessly and blindly in utter terror. The pain he had eluded all his life had caught him between four walls. And he was bruising himself against walls and furniture while she stood there mute and compassionate. His terror so great that he did not sense her pity, and when she moved to open the window to allow him to escape he interpreted the gesture as a menace. To run away from his own terror he flew wildly against the window and crushed his feathers.

Don't flutter so blindly, my father!

She grew suddenly tired of seeing her father always in profile, of seeing him always walking on the edge of circles, always elusive. The fluidity, the evasiveness, the deviations made his life a shadow picture. He never met life full-face. His eyes never rested on anything, they were always in flight. His face was in flight. His hands were in flight. She never saw them lying still, but always curving like autumn leaves over a fire, curling and uncurling. Thinking of him she could picture him only in motion, either about to leave, or about to arrive; she could see better than anything else, as he was leaving, his back and the way his hair came to a point on his neck.

She wanted to bring her father out in the open. She was tired of his ballet dancing. She would struggle to build up a new relationship.

But he refused to admit he had been lying. He was pale with anger. No one ever doubted him before—so he said. To be doubted blinded him with anger. He was not concerned with the truth or falsity of the situation. He was concerned with the injury and insult she was guilty of, by doubting him.

"You're demolishing everything," he said.

"What I'm demolishing was not solid," she answered. "Let's make a new beginning. We created nothing together except a sand pile into which both of us sink now and then with doubts. I am not a child. I cannot believe your stories."

He grew still more pale and angry. What shone out of his angry eyes was pride in his stories, pride in his ideal self, pride in his delusions. And he was offended. He did not stop to ask himself if she were right. She could not be right. She could see that, for a moment at any rate, he believed implicitly in the stories he had told her. If he had not believed in them so firmly he would have been humiliated to see himself as a poor comedian, a man who could not deceive even his own daughter.

"You shouldn't be offended," she said. "Not to be able to deceive your own daughter is no disgrace. It's precisely because I have told you so many lies myself that I can't be lied to."

"Now," he said, "you are accusing me of being a Don Juan."

"I accuse you of nothing. I am only asking for the truth."

"What truth?" he said, "I am a moral being, far more moral than you."

"That's too bad. I thought we were above questions of good and evil. I am not saying you are bad. That does not concern me. I am saying only that you are *false* with me. I have too much intuition."

"You have no intuition at all concerning me."

82

"That might have affected me when I was a child. Today I don't mind what you think of me."

"Go on," he said. "Now tell me, tell me I have no talent, tell me I don't know how to love, tell me *all that your mother used to tell me.*"

"I have never thought any of these things."

But suddenly she stopped. She knew her father was not seeing her any more, but always that judge, that past which made him so uneasy. She felt as if she were not herself any more, but her mother, her mother with a body tired with giving and serving, rebelling at his selfishness and irresponsibility. She felt her mother's anger and despair. For the first time her own image fell to the floor. She saw her mother's image. She saw the child in him who demanded all love and did not know how to love. She saw the child incapable of an act of protection, strength, or self-denial. She saw the child hiding behind her courage, the same child hiding now under Laura's protection. She was her mother telling him again that as a human being he was a failure. And perhaps she had told him too that as a musician he had not given enough to justify his limitations as a human being. All his life he had been playing with people, with love, playing *at* love, playing *at* being a pianist, playing *at* composing. Playing because to no one or nothing could he give his whole soul.

There were two regions, two tracts of land, with a bridge in between, a slight, fragile bridge like the Japanese bridges in the miniature Japanese gardens. Whoever ventured to cross the bridge fell into the abyss. So it was with her mother. She had fallen through and been drowned. Her mother thought he had a soul. She had fallen there in that space where his emotions reached their limit, where the land opened in two, where circles fell open and rings were unsoldered.

Was it her mother talking now? She was saying: "I am only asking you to be honest with yourself. I admit when I lie, but you never admit it. I am not asking for anything except that you be real."

"Now say I am superficial."

"At this moment you are. I wanted you to face me and be truthful."

He paced up and down, pale with anger.

It seemed to her that her father was not quarreling with her but with his own past, that what was coming to light now was his underlying feeling of guilt towards her mother. If he saw in her now an avenger it was only because of his fear that his daughter might accuse him too. Against her judgment he had erected a huge defense: the approbation of the rest of the world. But in himself he had never quite resolved the right and the wrong. He, too, was driven now by a compulsion to say things he never intended to say, to make her the symbol of the one who had come to punish, to expose his deceptions, to prove his worthlessness.

And this was not the meaning of her struggle with him. She had not come to judge him but to dissolve the falsities. He feared so much that she had come to say: "the four persons you abandoned in order to live your own life, to save yourself, were crippled," that he did not hear her real words. The scene was taking place between two ghosts.

Her father's ghost was saying: "I cannot bear the slightest criticism. Immediately I feel judged, condemned."

Her own ghost was saying: "I cannot bear lies and deceptions. I need truth and sincerity."

They could not understand each other. They were gesticulating in space. Gestures of despair and anger. Her father pacing up and down, angry because of her doubts of him, forgetting that these doubts were well founded, forgetting to ask himself if she was right or not. And she in despair because her father would not understand, because the fragile little Japanese bridge between the two portions of his soul would not hold her even for a moment, she walking with such light feet, trying to bring messages from one side to another, trying to make connections between the real and the unreal.

She could not see her father clearly any more. She could see only the hard profile cutting the air like a swift stone ship, a stone ship moving in a sea unknown to human beings, into regions made of granite rock. No more water, or warmth, or flow between them. All communication paralyzed by the falsity. Lost in the fog. Lost in a cold, white fog of falsity. Images distorted as if they were looking through a glass bowl. His mouth long and mocking, his eyes enormous but empty in their transparency. Not human. All human contours lost.

And she thinking: I stopped loving my father a long time ago.

What remained was the slavery to a pattern. When I saw him I thought I would be happy and exalted. I pretended. I worked myself up into ecstasies. When one is pretending the entire body revolts. There come great eruptions and revolts, great dark ravages, and above all, a joylessness. A great, bleak joylessness. Everything that is natural brings joy. He was pretending too—he had to win me as a trophy, as a victory. He had to win me away from my mother, had to win my approbation. Had to win me because he feared me. He feared the judgment of his children. And when he could not win me he suffered in his vanity. He fought in me his own faults, just as I hated in him my own faults.

Certain gestures made in childhood seem to have eternal repercussions. Such was the gesture she had made to keep her father from leaving, grasping his coat and holding on to it so fiercely that she had to be torn away. This gesture of despair seemed to prolong itself all through her life. She repeated it blindly, fearing always that everything she loved would be lost.

It was so hard for her to believe that this father she was still trying to hold on to was no longer real or important, that the coat she was touching was not warm, that the body of him was not human, that her breathless, tragic desire had come to an end, and that her love had died.

Great forces had impelled her towards symmetry and balance, had impelled her to desert her father in order to close the fatal circle of desertion. She had forced the hour-glass of pain to turn. They had pursued each other. They had tried to possess each other. They had been slaves of a pattern, and not of love. Their love had long ago been replaced by the other loves which gave them life. All those parts of the self which had been tied up in a tangle of misery and frustration had been loosened imperceptibly by life, by creation. But the feelings they had begun with twenty years back, he of guilt and she of love, had been like railroad tracks on which they had been launched at full speed by their obsessions.

Today she held the coat of a dead love.

This had been the nightmare—to pursue this search and poison all joys with the necessity of its fulfillment. To discover that such fulfillment was not necessary to life, but to the myth. It was the myth

85

which had forbidden them to deny their first ideal love or to recognize its illusory substance. What they called their destiny—the railroad track of their obsessions.

At last she was entering the Chinese theater of her drama and could see the trappings of the play as well as the play itself, see that the settings were made of the cardboard of illusion. She was passing behind the stage and could stop weeping. The suffering was no longer real. She could see the strings which ruled the scenes, the false storms and the false lightning.

She was coming out of the ether of the past.

The world was a cripple. Her father was a cripple. In striking out for his own liberty, to save his life, he had struck at her, but he had poisoned himself with remorse.

No need to hate. No need to punish.

The last time she had come out of the ether it was to look at her dead child, a little girl with long eyelashes and slender hands. She was dead.

The little girl in her was dead too. The woman was saved. And with the little girl died the need of a father.

The Voice

DJUNA is lying down in a cell-shaped room of the tallest hotel in the City, in a building shooting upward like a railroad track set for the moon. A million rooms like cells, all exactly alike, and reaching in swift confused layers towards the moon. The rapid birds of elevators traverse the layers with lightning flashes of their red and white eyes signaling UP or DOWN, to the sun terraces, the observation towers, the solarium, or the storage rooms in the underground. All the voices of the world captured by the radio wires in this Babel tower, and even when the little buttons are marked *off* this music of all the languages continues to seep through the walls. The people riding up and down the elevators are never permitted to crash through the last ceiling into pure space and never allowed to pierce through the ground floor to enter the demonic regions below the crust of the earth. When they reach the highest tip they swoop down again back to the heavy repose in darkness. For Djuna the elevator does not stop at the sun terraces. She is certain it will pass beyond and through the ceiling, as she does with her feelings, explode in a fuse of ascension. When it stops dead on the ground floor she feels a moment of anguish; it will not stop here but bury itself below, where there is hysteria and darkness, wells, prisons, tombs.

Passing through the carpeted hallways, she can hear the singing, the weeping, the quarrels and confessions seeping out. Her footsteps are not heard in this convent of adulteries. The chambermaid is passing, carrying old newspapers, magazines, cigarette butts, breakfast left-overs. The boy is running with telegrams, special deliveries and telephone messages. He passes and with him a knife thrust of icy wind angrily banging the doors opened on intimate lives. Trays of food for the lovers and for the unloved. The house detective.

Merely passing down the halls noiselessly over the carpeted floor Djuna is aware of confessions seeping out. The elevators disgorge people feverishly eager to confess. They ask for the room of the modern priest, where a man in an armchair is listening to the unfaithful lying on the divan, looking down at them, with his own face against the light. Looking down at them to keep fresh in him the wound of compassion. When the glance rests on human beings from this position, where he can see the frailty of the hair, how it parts, falls, where it thins, where he can see the brow like a sharp landslide, discover the delicacy of the skin as it alone reveals itself when watched obliquely, all men seem in need of protection. From where he looks all noses slant without audacity, point without impertinence, merely a tender root to the mouth. The eyes are covered by weary eyelids, their motion slower when watched from above, a curtain of hyper-sensitive skin lowered with the gravity of sleep or death. Without the thrusting light-duel of the eyes, without the glaze and fervor of expression, courage, cruelty, humor, all men look crucified, passive, covering painful secrets. The mouth without its sensual openness, its breath, appears like a target mark, a vulnerable opening, a wound in the human being through which all his sorrows run hysterically.

The man listening to confessions is confined to his armchair and he sees them all struggling, defeated, wounded, crippled. They are laying themselves open before him, demanding to be condoned, absolved, forgiven, justified. They want this Voice coming from a dark armchair, a substitute for God, for the confessor of old.

Djuna, lying down, remembers all this that she has lived, and that so many others are living after her. This talk in the dark with one who becomes part of herself, who answers all the doubts in her. This man without identity, the Voice of all she did not know but which was in her to bring to light. The Voice of the man who was helping her to be born again.

He was taking her slowly back to the beginning, and this talking to a man she could not see was like a dialogue with a Djuna much greater than the everyday Djuna, a Djuna she felt at times as clearly as one feels the pushing of the wind on street corners. The larger Djuna pushing the smaller one to act and speak greatness, not smallness or doubt or fear. The Voice had unearthed this larger Djuna, had confronted her with her desires, permitted them to fuse. Before this they lay separate with an abyss of yearning and hunger between them, one the smaller Djuna in a world she feared as tragic, the other the larger Djuna in a world she no longer feared. The Voice had spoken to dispel the turmoil in her, the dissonances, and the divisions: "I want to reconcile you to yourself." As if she had grown into two irreconcilable branches and so lost her strength.

"There is something wrong with me. I want to live only with the intimate self of the other. I only care about the intimate self. I hate to see people in the world, their masks, their falsities, their surrender to the world, their resemblance to others, their promiscuity. I only care about the secret self. I only want the dream and the isolation. I have the fear that everyone is leaving, moving away, that love dies in an instant. I look at the people walking in the street, just walking, and I feel this: they are walking, *but they are also being carried away*. They are part of a current. Each moment that is passing takes them somewhere else. I confuse the moods which change and pass with the people themselves. I see them carried into eddies, always moving out of some state they will never return to, I see them *lost*. They do not walk in circles, back to where they started, but they walk out and beyond in some irretrievable way—too fast—towards the end. And I feel myself standing there; I cannot move with them. I seem to be standing and watching this current passing and I am left behind. Why have I the feeling they all pass like the day, the leaves, the moods of climate, into death?"

"Because you are standing still and measuring time by your immobility, the others seem to run too fast towards an end. If you were living and running with them, you would cease to be aware of this death that is actually in you because you are watching."

"I stand for hours watching the river downtown. What obsesses me is the debris. I look at the dead flowers floating, petals completely opened, the life sucked out of them, flowers without pistils. Punctured rubber dolls bobbing up and down like foetuses. Boxes full of wilted vegetables, bottles with broken tops. Dead cats. Corks. Bread that looks like entrails. These things haunt me. The debris. When I watch people it is as if at the same time I saw the discarded parts of themselves. And so I can't see their motions except as acts which lead them faster and faster to the waste, the end, to the river where it will be thrown out. The faster they walk the streets, the faster they move towards this mass of debris. That is how I see them, caught by a current that carries them off."

"Only because you are standing still. If you were in the current, in love, in ecstasy, the motion would not show just its death aspect. You see what life throws out because you stand outside, shut out from the ferment itself. What is burned, used, is not regretted by anyone who *is* the fire consuming all this. If you were on fire you would enjoy throwing out what was dead. You would fight for the lightness of your movements. It is not living too fast and abandoning oneself that carries one towards death, but not moving. Then everything deteriorates. When parts of yourself die they are only like leaves. What refuses to live in you will become like cells through which the blood does not pass. The blood must pass. There must be change. When you are living you seek the change; it is only when you stop that you become aware of death."

Djuna walked out into the street, blind with the rush of memories. She stood in the center of the street eddies, and suddenly she knew the whole extent of her fear of flowing, of yielding, of depending on another. Suddenly she began walking faster than whoever was walking beside her, to feel the exultation of passing them. The one who does not move feels abandoned, and the one who loves and weeps and yields feels he is living so fast the debris cannot catch up with him. She was moving faster than the slowly flowing rivers carrying detritus. Moving, moving. Flowing, flowing, flowing. When she was watching, everything that moved seemed to be moving away, but when moving, this was only a tide, and the self turning, rotating, was feeding the rotation of desire.

It is as if she were in an elevator, shooting up and down. Hundreds of floors of sensations varying faster than temperature. Up into the sun garden, no floors above. Deliverance. A bower of light. Proximity to faith. At this height she finds something to lean on. Faith. But the red lights are calling: Down. The elevator coming down so swiftly brings her body to the concert floor. But her breath is caught midway, left in midheaven. Now she is breathing music, in which all anger dissolves. It is not the swift changes of floor which made her dizzy, but that parts of her body, of her life, are passing into every floor, into the lives of others. All that passes into the room of the Voice he pours back now into her, to deliver himself of the weight. She follows the confessions, each anguish is repeated in her. The resonance is so immense, resonance to wind, to lament, to pain, to desires, to every nuance of sensibility, so enormous the resonance, beyond the entire hotel, the high vault of sky and the black bowl of hysteria, that she cannot hear the music. She cannot listen to the music. Her being is brimming, spilling over, cannot contain its own knowledge. The music spills out, overflows, meets with the overfullness, and she cannot receive it. She is saturated. For in her it never dies. No days without music. She is like an instrument so tuned up, so exacerbated, that without hands, without players, without leadership, it responds, it breathes, it emits the continuous melody of sensibility. Never knew silence. Even in the darkest grottoes of sleep. So the concerts of the Hotel Chaotica Djuna cannot hear without exploding. She feels her body like an instrument which gives its strongest music when it is used as a body. Ecstasy reached only in the orchestra, music and sensuality traversing walls and reaching ecstasy. The orchestra is made with fullness, and only fullness rises to God. The soloist talks only to his own soul. Only fullness rises.

Like the fullness of the hotel. No matter what happened in each room, what diversions, distortions, hungers, incompletions, when Djuna reaches the highest floor, the alchemy is complete.

The telephone rang and there was someone downstairs waiting to see the Voice. It was urgent. This someone came up, shaking an umbrella dripping with melted snow. She entered his room walking sideways like a crab, and bundled in her coat as if she were a package, not a body. Between each two words there was a hesitancy. In each gesture a swing intended to be masculine, but as soon as she sat on the couch, looking up at the Voice, flushed with timidity, saying: "shall I take off my shoes and lie down," he knew already that she was not masculine. She was deluding herself and others about it. He was even more certain while watching her take off her shoes and uncover her very small and delicate feet. Not that the feet were an indication, but that he felt the woman in her through her feet, through her hands. They transmitted a woman current. The simple act of taking off her shoes betrayed that her caresses were those of a girl, girls in school arousing but the surface of each other's feminine senses and believing when they had traveled on lakes of gentle sensation that they had penetrated the dark, violent center of woman's response. All this he knew, and he was not surprised when she opened with: "I find it hard to confess to you, I am a pervert, I've had a lot of affairs with women." He wanted to smile. He could have smiled, she could not see him, but he could see her passing her delicate girl hand through the strands of her heavy hair with gestures meant to be heavy with disaster and dark implications. She could not, with any of her words, charge the atmosphere of the room as she meant to, with the darkness of her acts. The atmosphere continued delicate like her hands and feet. No matter what she was saying about her last love affairs, it was all permeated with innocence. She spoke breathlessly, with little repetitions and light gasps of awe and surprise at herself.

"I loved Hazel so, I was swallowed up by her, just as before that I loved Georgia, and she could do anything with me. I would even help her to see her lovers, I would do anything she asked me. She got tired of me, and I went off alone to Holland, and I could not play the violin any more, I wanted to die. I made love to other women, but it was not the same. What terrible things I have done in my life, you can't imagine. I don't know what you will think. I can't see your face and that bothers me. I can't tell you because maybe you won't want to see me any more. Georgia told me one lies down and talks; it is like talking to oneself except that this Voice comes and explains everything and it stops hurting. I feel fine here lying down, but I am ashamed of so many things and I think they are very bad things I did, this sleeping with women, and other things. I killed a woman who got married. It was in my birthplace, in the South. She got married and then died the night of the wedding, and *I did it.* I thought all the time before the wedding that she ought not to love a man, there is no tenderness in men, and then I thought of the blood, and I prayed she should die rather than be married, and so I wished it, and she died. And I am sure it was my fault. But there is something much worse than this. It happened in Paris. I was working at the violin, I remember. My room was on the level with the street and the windows were open; I was playing away, and suddenly, I don't know why, I looked at the bow and looked at it for a long while and I was taken with a violent desire to pass it between my legs, as if I were the violin, and I don't know why I did it, and suddenly I saw people laughing outside. . . . I nearly died of shame. You will never tell this to anyone? I can't tell what you are thinking about me. When I don't know what people think I always imagine they are laughing at me, criticising me. I don't feel that you condemn me, I feel good here, lying down. I feel that at last I am getting some terrible things out, getting rid of them maybe, maybe I will be able to forget them, like the time I gave a little boy an enema with a straw, and I thought I had injured him for life, and a few years after that he got sick and died, and I didn't dare walk through the town because I was sure it was the enema that did it. Don't you think it was? I don't know why I did that. I wish I could see your face. I want revenge above all, because I was operated on, and I was not told why; I was told it was for appendicitis, and when I got well I found out I had no more woman's parts, and I feel that men will never want me because I can't have a child. But that is good because I don't like men, they have no tenderness. Not being able to have a child—that means I am a cripple; men won't love me. But I'm sure I wouldn't like it with a man—I tried how it felt once with a toothbrush, and I didn't like it. I had the funniest dream just before coming to you; I had opened my veins and I was introducing mercury into them, into each vein at the finger tip. Why can I never be happy? I am always thinking when I'm in love that it will come to an end, just like now I think if I don't find more things to tell you, I won't be able to come again, and I am afraid of this coming to an end, afraid you will not think me sick enough."

A week later, ten days later, she is lying down and talking to the Voice:

"Last night I was able to play. I felt you standing over me like an enormous shadow, and I could see your large signet ring flashing, and what was stranger than all this, I smelled the odor of your cigar suddenly in the middle of the street. How can you explain this, walking casually through a street, I smelled your cigar and that made me breathe deeply; I always walk with my shoulders hunched up, you've noticed it; I walk like a man; I am sure I am a man after all, because when I was a child I played like a boy; I hated to dress up in pretty things and I hated perfume. I don't understand why the smell of your cigar, which reminds me of my talks with you, made me want to breathe deeply. It's very funny. I haven't thought about Hazel for the last few days; maybe I don't love her any more; I only feel I love her when we are separating, when I see her going off on a train; then I feel terrible, terrible. Otherwise I am not very sure that I love her, really. I feel nothing when she is there, we quarrel a lot, that is all. With Georgia it was different, she made me feel she was there: Lillian, do this for me; Lillian, do that for me; Lillian, telephone for me; Lillian, carry my music. She was always deathly ill; I had to run around for her all the time; she was always dying, but always well enough to receive lovers. Always clinging to me, talking to me about her great loneliness, her love affairs. This talking to you is the most wonderful thing that ever happened to me. How strange it is to talk absolutely sincerely as it comes, to say everything in one's head. I am getting well, but I don't want you to send me away. When I was a child I always wanted to go to Africa. I had a scrapbook all about Africa, with maps, timetables, boat sailings, information, pictures of airplanes and of the boats that could take me there. My school was very far away, I had to walk for two hours, and I called it Africa. I would set out for it all prepared for a trip. I liked going to school because it was Africa, and I thought about it at night. And then they built a new school right next to my home, five minutes away, and I never went to school again. I was expelled; my father never forgave me; he was so mad he threw a knife out of the window and it hit our mare in the leg and that made a terrible impression on me; it was my fault too. Yesterday when I left you I was thinking about God, and what do you think happened to me? Walking out of the hotel I stumbled on the steps and I found myself kneeling on the sidewalk, and I did not mind it at all; it was wonderful, so many times I have wanted to kneel on the sidewalk, and I had never dared, and now thinking about you and what I could say to you the next time so you won't think I'm cured yet and send me away I felt that I have something now which you can't take from me, ever since I came here I have a feeling so warm and sweet and life-giving which belongs to me, I know you gave it to me, but it is inside of me now, and you can't take it away."

Mischa came to the Voice limping, but he only talked about his hand. He could no longer play the cello. His hand was stiff. He was mute about his leg.

His mother had been a Cossack woman who rode horseback. His father had been obsessed with hunting. Mischa himself had never wanted women except when they wore red dresses, and then he felt like biting them. Women seemed to him something soft and blind, something to hide into. When he saw a woman he wanted to become small and hide in her. He used to call his mother in Russian, his Holy Secret.

His hand had been twisted, cramped for many years. He held it out to show the Voice. He talked constantly about his hand, how it felt, if it was stiffer today than yesterday. He had played the cello when he was very young. He had been a child prodigy. He remembered early concerts and his mother afterwards taking him between her large, strong horsewoman's knees and caressing him with pleasure because he had played well. His mother had been like no woman he had ever seen. She had very long black hair which she liked to wear down when she was at home, a sort of forest of black hair in which he would hide his face. His good-night kiss had never been anywhere but inside this black hair. Absolute blackness then, the hair tickling his eyelashes and getting inside his mouth. Hair so violent and strong, with a smell that made him dizzy, hair that entwined itself around him. His mother had looked like a Medusa. Her hair must have been made of snakes, her face somehow fixed into one expression. It seemed to him that her eyes had never blinked. And the voice of a man and a bass laughter. A laughter that had lasted longer than any he had ever heard. He could hear it from his bed at night. He had dreamed of climbing with the help of his mother's long, heavy hair to a place where his father could not reach him. His father, all in leather, armed with guns, carrying wounded animals, dripping with blood, surrounded by dogs. It seemed to Mischa that he had found his mother's voice in the cello.

For days after this Mischa did not talk. He could not play the cello, he could not move his hand freely, and there were things he didn't want the Voice to know. But he felt that the Voice was watching him, feeling his way deftly into his secrets. He felt that the Voice was not convinced at all that it was the hand which caused Mischa's suffering. He felt slowly surrounded by intricate questions, pressed closer by unexpected associations. He felt like a criminal, but he could not remember the crime. The Voice enveloped him in questions. Mischa felt a great anguish, as if he had committed a crime and were now concealing it. And he could not remember what it was. He felt the place where it was buried. What was buried? There, under the flesh, at the very bottom of murky well of clay, there was something buried. Something which the Voice pushed him towards. An image. What? An image of his magnificent Medusa mother standing in her room. He was a little boy of eight. He had not been able to sleep. He had limped quietly to her room and knocked faintly at her door. She had not heard his knock. He had opened the door very slowly. He knew his father was not there, that he was out hunting. His mother was standing before him, very tall, wearing a long white nightgown. And on this white robe there was a blood stain. He had seen the stain. He had smelled the blood on her. He had cried out hysterically. He ran out of her room to look for the father. He picked up a riding whip. His father was returning from the hunt. He was standing at the door, taking off his leather coat, laying down his gun. There was a bloodstain on his sleeve. The animals he had killed were lying in the hall. The dogs were still barking, outside. Mischa went up to his father and struck him, struck at the man who had stained his mother's white robe with blood, who had hunted her as he hunted the animals.

As he told this he held up before him the stiffened hand. He thought the Voice would speak about the hand, but the Voice asked him: "And the lameness?"

Mischa winced and turned his face away. Behind what he had told lay his secret. Behind the facade of the image, the scene which he saw so clearly, lay a terrain of broken, cutting fragments, and on this a dead leg, like some discarded object, but not buried. It had always lain there, unburied. Dead. He was more aware of it than anything about his life. The dead leg rested right across the whole body, wooden. He had nailed his hand on it. Life, colors, music, women—all were hung around this dead leg, like votive offerings. There had never been any Mischa, Mischa was in that leg, imprisoned, bound in it. The pain of lameness, of knowing, even as a child, that one carries a fragment of death in one. To live with a dead fragment of oneself. The fierce graspingness of death already setting in. To be crippled, humiliated, left out of games, not to be able to ride horseback. The lameness concealed at concerts, but not before women. The wounded look in the fixed gaze of the mother when she watched him walk. Her love for him was not joyous, but heavy with compassion. When she kissed others she radiated an animal pride, her nostrils quivered. When she kissed Mischa it was as if part of her died at the very touch of him, in answer to the part in him that was dead. Mischa trembled when he had to walk across a room. He hated women because of his lameness, because they too closed a fierce part of themselves when they approached him, made themselves more tender, more attenuated, and looked at him as his mother had looked at him. He was ashamed. So terribly ashamed. The Voice said very gently: "You preferred to offer your hurt hand to people's eyes. You offered the whole world your hurt hand. You talked about your hand. You showed your hand so no one would notice the lameness. The hand did not shame you. The hand that struck your father seemed to you rightfully, humanly punished by immobility."

Mischa was weeping, his face turned to the wall. Now that he looked at the lameness, the leg seemed to become less dead, less separate from him. The leg was not so heavy, not so gruesome, as the secret of the pain he had enclosed in it, his fear and pain before the leg. Every nerve and cell in him tense with the fear of discovery, tense with rigid pretending, dissolved in new tears before the fact which appeared smaller, less dark, less oppressive. The crime and the secret did not seem so great as when he had watched over its tomb. The pain was not so much like a monster now, but a simple, human sorrow. With the tears the great tension all through the body softened. He was a cripple. But he had committed no crime. He had struck his father, but his father had laughed at the scene, and his mother too. They had hurt him more than he had hurt them. The tears were like a river carrying away the tension. The walls he had erected, the nightmares he had buried in his being, the tightness of fear, the knots in his nerves, all dissolving. Everything was washed away. And the big knot in his hand, that was loosening too. It was the same knot. The muted hand that could no longer draw his mother's voice out of the cello. The static hand that could no longer strike. The crippled hand for the world to see, while the real shamed Mischa walked surreptitiously before them hoping to conceal his dead leg from the world.

Exaltation lifted him from the couch, out of the room. He was running out of this room filled with knowing eyes, through the softly carpeted hall, passing all the rooms filled with revelations, to the red lights that bore him down to the street.

In the street he did not feel the sea of ice and snow. The warmth was in him like a fire that would never go out. He was singing.

In the underground drugstore, Djuna sat eating at the counter. The young man was mixing his sallies with the drinks: "Are you a show girl too?" he asked her. The sea elephant, owner of the place, swam heavily towards her with a box: "I kept this box for you; I thought you would like it. It smells good." The sea elephant sank behind the counter, behind waves of perfume bottles, talcum powder, candy packages, cigar boxes. She was left with the sandalwood box in her arms.

She carried it through the lobby. The lobby was full of waiting people lumped there, waiting without impatience, reading, mumbling, meditating, sleeping.

Every time she passed through the lobby her throat tightened. Behind every chair, every palm tree, every sofa, every face half-seen in the dim light of the lobby, she feared to recognize someone she knew. *Someone out of the past.* She could repeat to herself as she passed that they were all lost, that in the enormous city they had lost her tracks. She had crossed the ocean, destroyed their addresses. Stretches of long years and of sea lay between that first half of her life and this. The city had swallowed them. Yet each time she crossed the lobby she felt the same apprehension. She feared the return of the past. They sat in the lobby waiting, waiting for a crevice, a passageway back into her life. Waiting to introduce themselves again. They had left their names at the desk. So many of them.

They were waiting to be admitted. They wanted to come upstairs and enter her present life. Djuna herself did not understand why this should be such an intolerable idea. Perhaps not so much their coming back, if they came for a visit and sat in a chair and talked. But they might act like a sea rushing forward and sweeping her back again into the undertows of early darkness. Surely she had thrown them out with the broken toys, but they sat there, threatening to sweep her back. Stuffed, with glass eyes, from a slower world, they look at her on this other level of swifter rhythms, and they reach with dead arms around her. She wanted to escape them in elevators which flew up and down like great, swift birds of variety and change. Moving among many rooms, many people, among great secrets and feverish happenings. Their tentacles like the tentacles of the earth waiting for the return to where she came from. Could all escape be an illusion? That was her fear, seeing duplicates of the people who had filled her early world.

She would go and have her hair washed, which was as good as weeping. The water runs softly through the roots of the being, like warm rain, and washes away everything. One falls into rhythm again. She would have her hair washed and feel this simple flow of life through the hair. She passed into the hair-washer's cubicle, out of the lobby of the waiting past.

Djuna was soon poised again on the threshold, faced with the same fear of traversing the lobby. There was a moment of extraordinary silence in the enormous hotel: she could not tell if it was in her. A moment of extraordinary slowness of motion. Then came a dull, powerful sound outside. A heavy sound but dull, without echo. Djuna felt the shock in her body. The shock traversed the entire hotel, the silence and the panic were communicated, transmitted with miraculous speed. All at once, it seemed, without words, everyone knew what had happened. A woman had thrown herself from a window and fallen on the garage roof. Thrown herself from the twenty-fifth floor. She was dead, of course, dead, and with a five-month child inside her. She had taken a room in the hotel in the morning, given a false name. Had stayed five hours without moving

99

from the room. And then thrown herself out with the child in her. The sound, the dead heavy body sound, resonant still in the structure of the hotel, in the bodies of the people communicating this image one to another. Djuna could see her bleeding and open. The impact. Fallen, fallen so quickly back to the bottom. Birds fell this way when they died in the air. Had she died in the air? When had she died? Ascension high, to fall from greater heights and be sure of death. Loneliness, for five hours in a room with this child who could not answer her if she questioned, if she doubted, if she feared. . . .

The radios were turned on again. People moved fast again, normally. The silence had been in everyone, for one second. Then everyone had closed his eyes and moved faster, up and down. One must get dizzy. One must move. Move.

Djuna sat in the room of the Voice. The little man no one ever saw, he was standing by the window.

"Look," he said, "they are skating in the Park. It is Sunday. The band is playing. I could be walking in the snow with the band playing. That is happiness. When I had happiness I did not recognize it, or feel it. It was too simple. I did not know I had it. I only know it now when I am sitting here confined to this armchair and listening to confessions. My body is cramped. I want to do the things they do. At most I am allowed to watch. I am condemned to see through a perpetual keyhole every intimate scene of their life. But I am left out. Sometimes I want to be taken in. I want to be desired, possessed, tortured too."

Djuna said: "You can't stop confessing them, you can't stop. A woman killed herself, right there, under your window; that noise you heard was the fall of her body. She was pregnant. And she was alone. That is why she killed herself."

"I listen to them all. They keep coming and coming. I thought at first that only a few of them were sick. I did not know that they were all sick and bursting with secrets. I did not know there was no end to their coming. Did you ever walk through the lobby? I have a feeling that down there they are all waiting to be confessed. They all have more to say than I have time to hear. I could sit here until I die and even then there will be women throwing themselves out of the window on the same floor on which I live."

Lilith was waiting for the steamer bringing her brother from India. She watched the people stepping off the gangplank. She feared she would not recognize him. When he had left he was a boy. A boy in a plaster cast of hardness, of dissimulation. Intent on defending himself against all invasion by others, against feeling, against softness, against himself. A boy swinging between violent, brutal acts, and fits of weeping like a woman. Would she recognize the compressed mouth, the ice-blue eyes, the pose of nonchalance, the briefness of speech, the tension and the sudden breaks in the tension? A boy in a plaster cast of hardness. Untouchable. At times she suspected that he had refused to recognize her presence in him. Perhaps it was he walking there, so rigid in his clothes. No. So many people, so many valises, trunks, confusions, greetings. And then suddenly there was no one else passing down the gangplank.

Lilith stopped one of the stewards: "Do you know Eric Pellan? Can you tell me if he's sick? I can't find him."

The steward promised to go and see. Lilith imagined Eric lying in his bunk, sick. She waited, already suffering, as she suffered when he was small and in trouble. The steward returned: "I have found him," he said. "He's not sick, but his papers are not quite in order, so he can't step off the boat until tomorrow morning. He wants you to come on board."

The eyes watching behind eyeglasses. They faced each other without words. There was a break in their pause as if the bodies would break at the shock of their meeting. Then he smiled brusquely, and the talk broke through the barrier of fifteen years.

"You look swell," he said. "Are you as bossy as you were? Remember how you wanted to do the fighting for me? You wouldn't let me fight my own battles with the boys. You came with an umbrella and beat them. They laughed at me for having a sister fighting for me. I had to go far away to get away from you. You look swell! Who do you fight for now? Who do you help cross the street? Who do you stop the traffic for now, with insults at the drivers? You look swell, much sweller, much sweller than before. But you can't boss me now."

All the passengers had left the boat but a few of the crew and the purser who was adding numbers and listing names on long sheets of green paper behind his barred window. A few of the crew were cleaning the cabins and decks. They had drawn the curtains, covered tile chairs and couches and the pianos. They had waxed the floors, turned over the mattresses, folded up the blankets, put out the lights. The enormous parlors and lounge rooms looked ghostly. So many chairs in rows with stiffened arms open on emptiness. The ship anchored in earth, it seemed, so steady it was. Room after room without dust, without lights. Funereal. The mirrors reflecting nothing but a brother and sister walking through the enormous ship, through a labyrinth of linoleum hallways, passing doors opening into a million empty cabins. The bunks like skeletons, showing the springs and the box-like edges. Silence. . . . A sudden shadow of a sailor polishing the brass knobs. Brother and sister walking through a city of cabins. No smell in the kitchen, no rolling and swaying or cracking of wood. A carcass at rest. No music in the salons, no glitter of silverware chiming in the dining rooms. Repose of furniture, windows, lights. A funereal watch of covered chairs. A dead backstage. No vestige of the people who passed. Clean.

Brother and sister stranded. Not allowed to land, they walked on a frontier not marked on the marine or earthly charts. Frontiers of memory. The anchor dug deep into the sandy marshes of memory. Here in the skeleton of the marine monster, with its empty windows unblinking, its empty decks, empty salons, deserted by the musicians and sailors, beyond the earth and beyond the sea, they sit before a banquet of memories. The ship was the world of their childhood filled with indestructible games. He had carried his childhood to India, he had dyed it in foreign colors, he had bathed it in exotic music, burned it in unnameable fevers, choked it with strange incenses, strangled it in new loves, lost it in opium deliriums, buried it in Mahometan cemeteries. It had turned to ivory, to a mineral in his breast. The more they pressed down on it, the stronger the compression, the more it had gained in rarity, in fixity. A diamond lodged in the breast.

Brother and sister walking through the skeleton of the monstrous ship which had taken him away and brought him back with the same diamond lodged in the breast. Bathing in the acid of the past, they bared the bones unbleached and this diamond.

Their first imaginary voyage with chairs, tables, rags, was the most prolonged in all their existence. The ship they had boarded together at birth had never moved; they were locked in it forever, without passengers and without landing permits. All the other cabins empty, and they forever cursed to sail inside the static sea of their fantasies. Riveted to the shore of the past, forbidden to land, with the anchor set deep in rust.

Another day in the confessional. Lilith lying down and talking. Lilith watching the Voice with something like hostility, expecting him to say something dogmatic, some banality, some unsubtle generality. She wanted him to say it, because if he did he would be another man she could not lean on, and she would have to go on conquering herself and her own life alone. She was proud of her independence. She was waiting for the Voice to say something unsubtle that she could laugh at.

They were talking about Mischa. He told her that she was an obsession in Mischa's life. That he saw her as the mother, the sister, the most unattainable of women, and for this he wanted to conquer her, to free his manhood. Then she confessed how at first she had loved Mischa, but when she had felt his smallness, his way of hiding within women, she had felt protection but no desire. She had wanted to give him an illusion but feared not to be able to sustain it to the very end. She begged the Voice not to tell him the truth, which would wound him, but to tell Mischa *she* was a little mad. This would explain the change in her, put all the blame on herself, and Mischa might enjoy discovering there were other abnormal people in the world. The Voice agreed with her. He asked her if she did not mind other people thinking she was not normal. She hesitated and then:

"No, I don't mind. I like to think me puzzling, mystifying and unpredictable. I feel that I keep my real self a mystery."

The Voice laughed a little at this.

103

"I see you don't need any help at all, you are quite content, quite strong, quite able to manage your own life."

At these words Lilith began to tremble, and then she felt her attitude crumble, the facade crumbling all around her. She became intensely aware of her weakness, her need of another. She said nothing but the Voice understood and continued: "You have acted beautifully towards Mischa. As few women will act. In general women consider men as enemies, and they are glad when they can humiliate or demolish them."

"I could not hurt Mischa. Whenever I see him I remember the story he told me about his first sensual curiosity. His mother had discovered him weighing his sex in his hand, reflectively, had beaten him with a whip and left him locked up in the room. He wept hysterically, then quieted down and dipping a finger in the tears, he had written on the wall: evil boy. He waited for the words to vanish, but they seemed to remain like stains on the wall, and he grew hysterically afraid the words would never dry and that the whole city would know about his doings."

Lilith liked the way the Voice's questions crackled at her from all directions. He was behind her and she was not ashamed to speak of anything. At the same time she felt that she could not deceive him even by a shade of falsity, for he was so attentive to every hesitation, every inflection of the voice, every gesture she made, and especially the *silences*. Every silence put him on a new scent. He was really the hunter of secret thoughts. They would reach a blank wall. She would repeat: "I don't know. I don't remember. I don't think so." But the truth was apparent from what she felt at his words. Whenever something had hurt her, and he touched upon it, she felt a churning of feelings, a warning: *Here is the place.* He uncovered her wars against herself: "I see myself always too small or too large. I awake one day feeling small, and another day bursting with a power which makes me believe I can rule the whole world."

When he talked it was like a stirring of quicksands. She felt the whole sandy bottom of her life, a complete insecurity, rootlessness. He said perhaps she was a woman who was not the enemy of man, but she remembered days of great hatred for man. He talked about the unyieldingness and the fear. Fear of being hurt, he said. Why?

She did not know. How could man hurt her? He had hurt her already.

"My first feeling was that my father was not tied to anything. He was not tied to my mother, he was not tied to us, he was not tied to the women he made love to. He was tied to nothing. He was always leaving, forgetting, throwing out, betraying."

When she made this very simple statement Lilith felt the most intense anguish. She turned her head to look at the Voice and said: "I can't go on."

"You must go on."

"The first thing I saw was a father escaping from the mother. Running away from us, from the house. From everything. I saw my mother left maimed, like someone who had lost an arm. I saw our house sold and disrupted. It was like a deluge. Everything was carried away. The strange, mysterious atmosphere we lived in as children, our games which were like an enchantment from which we never freed ourselves: nothing was ever the same. I saw the furniture out in the garden being sold at auction. I saw my father leaving and sending postcards from all over the world. The world was immense, it seemed to me, and he was in all of it except the corner where he left us. He not only took himself away, but our faith in the marvelous too. The world of our childhood closed with his departure."

"All these departures, these upheavals, gave you a hatred of change. You, in your anger and pain, stood in the center and refused to move, decided to make a fixed core within you. You accepted outer change, but fought against it by creating an inner static groove. You would not move. Everything else around you could move, change, but you, because of your mistrust of pain and loss, refused to move. You would be the island, the fixed center. For fear of a second loss, a second abandon, a second wound. That is why you never again gave yourself, that is why you are cold. You are afraid of giving yourself wholly."

Lilith felt a deep anguish as he talked. She could not tell if the Voice was right or wrong, but she could feel with his words the invasion of a most painful secret. Exactly as if this set, tense, granite core of herself were being touched and found not to be granite. Found to

105

have nerves, sensibilities and memories. She remembered at this moment that when she heard that stones had a heartbeat, a kind of faint pulse which had never before been registered, she had cried out angrily: "how terrible, everything in the world feels. Exactly what I feared. That is why I am always so tender with everything. To think that even a stone can feel!"

And now the Voice was entering into this secret pain, exposing the vulnerability and the fear in her, and the anguish was immense.

Lilith said: "Now I hate you. You took away the little protection I had, the little cover I kept over things. I feel humiliated to have exposed myself. I who so rarely confess!"

"And why don't you confess?"

"It is always I who receive the confidences. People confess their doubts and fears to me. I am afraid of showing my weakness. Why? I think I will be less loved."

"Do you love those who expose their weakness? "

"Yes, even more. I feel them very near to me. I feel human and I love them."

"Then don't you think they might feel the same way towards you?"

"I feel I have been given another role, a non-human one. I don't know why."

"Because the father failed you. . . . You cannot depend on others. You prefer to be depended on."

Lilith went out in the street. She felt the day much softer on her skin. The snow was melting. It seemed to her that she let the day get nearer to her, permitted it to touch her. That before she had looked at the day like a stranger. Now she felt the day all over her body, the sensual touch of it. She was now like Djuna who felt everything with her skin, her finger tips, her hair, the soles of her feet. Djuna was like a plant. Every time Lilith saw Djuna she felt this strange, continuous, vibrating life of plants and water. There was a nobility, a constant motion and reverberation.

Lilith had never imagined this until today. She was breathing with the day, moving with the wind, in accord with it, with the sky, undulating like water, flowing and stirring to the life about her, opening like the night. What had happened? Only the Voice saying to her: Don't you love those who confess to you? Don't you love

106

their blindness, their blunders, their weakness? When they talk to you about their crimes, don't you dissolve with a human passion, with a desire to carry them, share everything that happens to them? Yes, yes, cried Lilith. Then *you* . . . Why do you . . . But then if I, Lilith, if I leaned, the others would find nothing there to rest on. If I became human, then where will the others go? They would go to the Voice, more of them. If I show anything but this strength, what will happen to them? He asks me what will happen to me; I don't think I care much what happens to me. I have a feeling that I am responsible for them. How restless he got, the Voice, when I asked him if he thought certain people had a destiny which forbade them to be human. I must have touched something which affected him. I will make him talk. I will question him.

But the Voice did not answer her questions. The Voice pried and prodded into her marriage.

The man Lilith had married was very simple. He had not found the way to woo her, to break down her resistance. Every night it had been the same flight, the same locked door against him, a hatred of his desire. She showed all her claws, her wild hair, her hatred of sex. Finally, one day they discussed it coolly. She asked him: "What is it like? Tell me." He did not know what to say, so he made a drawing. The drawing revolted her and frightened her all the more. She wouldn't even let him kiss her after the drawing. Finally he persuaded her to have it done by a doctor. She preferred the idea of a knife. It was a knife which first cut into her being.

"I tried to feel as a woman afterwards. It was a terrible thing, it was as if the knife had made me close forever rather than open, as if it had made me cold forever. There were times when I felt strong excitement in me, warmth, desire. I yielded without feeling to adventures. They all remained strangers to me. I never wanted to see them again. Do you think they killed the feeling in me that time? I can't bear this any more. I have a constant feeling that I'm living on the edge of something about to happen, and that I can never reach. My nerves are set for a climax of some kind. I feel tense and expectant. It is so agonizing that I begin to wish for a catastrophe which would relieve the expectancy. I wish for all the calamities, all the tragedies to happen at once. I want scenes, quarrels, tears, I want to be devoured, I want to strike at people. I feel restless. I can't stay

107

very long anywhere. I can't sit and I can't sleep. I always have this feeling that I must seek a relief from this waiting, a shattering moment before I can rest, sleep. As if death were waiting, death were pursuing me, watching me. The whole world arouses me, I feel love for people in the streets, music stirs me at all times like a caress; I desire violently, and I wait. I feel the storm coming, I feel the anguish, but everything continues the same, sluggish, without break, without lightning. Something in me wants to break, to explode. Instead, I have to take pleasure in breaking the lives of others. I am constantly seducing others, enchanting them, capturing them, while wishing they could do it to me. I want so much to be captured. Everyone obeys me, but they don't find the key to me. I like to feel their hearts beating faster, I like to see their eyes waver, their lips tremble, to feel the emotion in them. It is like food. I am fascinated by their feelings. I am like a huntress who does not want to kill, but I want to feel the wound. What do I expect? To be caught in the desire of the other and bathe in it. To burn. But I am always disappointed. No one can take possession of me. It is as if they were all blind, circling around me. I warm myself and then I become aware that the current is not passing through me. It is as if I were an idol of some kind. I always dream of this: I see myself standing very rigid, and I am covered with jewelry and luxuriant robes. I wear a crown. Do you think I will ever turn into a woman? I want to be shattered into bits. Yet at the same time I know I do everything to create my own inaccessibility. I wear strange clothes which estrange people. And then I hate them for failing to reach me. I know I create the legend. It is hard to explain, but I do have the feeling that I come from very far. While I sleep I know that many things have happened. I do not remember them all but I don't wake *near* everything. That is why sometimes when I come into a room I do not look at the people as if they were of my own race. It is true I feel they look at me and see this distant personage. I talk to them and I choose the most remote subject, the most remote from daily life. I feel compelled to do this, while at the same time I want warmth and simplicity. I feel alone. Sometimes they are taken with a furious madness to do violence to me, to clutch at me. But it's like a desire for a tabooed object, for a secret temple, for some forbidden person. For what is untouchable. And I, the woman inside of all this, I feel this. I feel I have created this personage and that I sit outside of her, lamenting because they are worshipping a sort of image, and they don't reach with simple, warm hands and touch me. It's as if I were outside this very costume, desiring and calling for simplicity, and at the same time a kind of fear compels me to continue acting. You are the only one I feel near to, you and Djuna, the only ones who don't make love to my shadow."

"But it is your own making. We are simply the ones who can't be mystified and entangled in your appearance. We are simply the ones who did not get lost in the labyrinth you create. You hide yourself and then you weep because people get lost in all this external form of your life. It's only locking doors against those who wish to come near, the same door that you locked against your husband."

Such simple words he said, yet Lilith left him feeling a great warmth towards him, something that resembled love. She was falling in love with the Voice. She felt that he was the subtle detective who made all these discoveries in her, who made her state the very nature of what hurt her. He liked the game of tracking down her most difficult thoughts. It was only after many detours that she could make these long revelations. It was as if he possessed her, somehow, in a way she could not explain to herself. There was a silent, subtle force in him. It was not in the words he said. It was something he exhaled. He confronted one with one's own self, naked, one's true self as it was at the beginning. He destroyed the deformations, one by one, the acquired disguises of the personality. It was like a return to the original self, a return to the beginning where everything was pure.

He took her back, with his questions and his probings, back to the beginning. She told him all she could remember about her father, ending with: "the need of a father is over."

The Voice said: "I am not entirely sure that the little girl in you ever died, or her need of a father. What am I to you?"

"The other night I dreamed you were immense, towering over everyone. You carried me in your arms and I felt no harm could come to me. I have no more fears since I talk to you like this every day. But lately I have become aware that it is you who are not happy. I think too of the way you play upon souls. It must give you a feeling of great power, the way they expose themselves."

"Power, yes . . . power. But every moment the human being in me is killed. I am not permitted any weaknesses. It is true that I could take people's great need of love and understanding and play upon it. When they open their secrets to me, they are in my power. But I want them to know me, and they don't. Even when they love me, it is a love that is not addressed to me. I remain anonymous. I am only allowed to watch the spectacle, but I am never allowed to enter. If I enter into a life I am still the oracle or the seer. You are the first one who has asked me a question about myself."

People came to him for strength; their image of him was of his tallness, his firmness, his wisdom. His strange phrases which acted on them like someone breaking their chains. Simple phrases. He defended them, supported them, transported them. An apocalyptic strength in him. Something above confusion and chaos. A total man, not made as they were of wavering moods, dispersed fragments, changes and contradictions. An alchemist who could always transmute the pain. The Sphinx who answered all questions. The one before whom one could become small again, in whom one could find a refuge. He lulled them, lifted them up out of whatever agonizing region they were trapped in. Brought them where they could live better, breathe better, love better, live in harmony with themselves, he reconciled them to the world, conquered the demons and ghosts haunting them. But when they look at the man inside the armor of impersonal phrases they find him smaller, older, different from their image. The little man rises, his shoulders are stooped, he shakes off the stiffness of his limbs, the cramp of the attentive echo, shakes the blood that was asleep during the trance of clairvoyance, shakes off the role imposed on him.

In their dreams they saw him as god, or as a demon. But always above. When the confession ended he was no longer above.

Lilith said: "I feel the real you behind the analyst. All you say comes out of you. No one else could act the same way towards human beings. It is not a system. It is your own goodness, your own compassion. I am sure they do not all use the same words, the same tone. There is magic in you."

"I am only a symbol."

"You are more than a symbol. I know separate and personal

things about you. I have watched you. You have a love of the absolute, a passion for extracting the essence."

"That's all very true."

"You have a gift for life which you have never used."

"I was not permitted to use it. I was not loved for myself but for my understanding, for the strength I gave. It was always unreal and false."

"I could say to you what you said to me: did you reveal your true self? Wasn't it you who insisted on wearing the mask of the analyst? You who became a Voice? An impersonal Voice? Look how you sit now, while we talk. You never move. You always sit in the same chair. I know nothing about you. Naturally, I can only attach myself to an image. I wish . . . I am going to ask you to do something very difficult. Suppose, just for once, that you lie here on the couch and I sit in your chair—like this—and now I'm you and you're me. What did you dream last night?"

She was laughing while she made him change places. He looked uneasy, bewildered.

"Why are you so uneasy?" she asked, "what are you afraid to reveal? Tell me what you are most ashamed to tell."

"Not to you, because you still need me, and while you need me I must remain a mystery to you."

"I don't need you."

"You do. Even what you're doing now is only because you need a victory over me. I made you confess, you want to make me confess. As soon as you find someone who has the key to you you want to reverse the roles. You can't bear to be discovered or dominated."

"You're wrong, you're utterly wrong," said Lilith violently. "I only did it because I am interested in you as a human being, because I am wondering about this man we all use and whom no one really knows."

"We'll see who is wrong," said the Voice, but this Voice was not as firm as when he sat with his back to the light.

The Voice is talking to Djuna:

"Do you think Lilith loves me? If Lilith loved me I would give up all this and begin a new life. I want to give up analysis. Otherwise I would go mad. Do you know what has happened to me during the last four days? Everything that I think of becomes the theme of the day, and all the people who come talk to me about the same thing. First I had a dream of jealousy. I was crazily jealous of someone, I don't know who. I awakened filled with a kind of fury and hatred as if someone were taking the woman I wanted away from me. I may have been jealous of Lilith, I don't know. But I awakened jealous. And then the people began to come, one after another. I had no more time to think over my dream. *But every one of them talked about jealousy.* First came a woman who was jealous of her husband's first wife, now dead. It was her own sister who had died, and whose husband had then married her. But he still loved her sister. The first time he took her he called out the name of the dead wife. He sought out the resemblances, he liked her to wear the same colors. And this woman felt it, and was tortured because she loved him. He lived in a dream, wrapped in the past. He took her without really taking her, as in a trance. She was in such despair that she thought of nothing else: how to kill his love for her dead sister, how to kill this other woman who had not died for him. She observed that he was very jealous. She sought out the men he was attached to, and gave herself to them, always in such a way that it would be known to him. And then he began to suffer. He became slowly aware of her, of her being loved by other men. She became more vivid in him through his hatred of her. By the presence of the pain and anger, he began to awaken to her, to her presence, nearness, seduction. He passed from long periods of dreaming to long moments of suffering. He lived with this violent consciousness of her sensual life. She would not let him touch her. Finally the pain became so intolerable that it aroused him to a violent awareness of her, desire for her; and in this fury somehow, the past was destroyed, like some vague dream. He became aware of the woman in her, her yieldings, her sensual responses, of their life in the present. This was the first story I heard in the morning. I was possessed with jealousy of Lilith, and everyone who came to me seemed possessed with jealousy. I felt my own jealousy in them, and it increased it, magnified it. I asked myself: what kind of feelings has Lilith towards me? Why has she become so vividly alive and why do I hate the way she gives herself? It seemed to me the world was full of jealousy, and it was contagious. It lay at the bottom of every nature. I saw everyone being jealous either in the past, the present or the future. One man talked to me continuously about scenes which had never taken place, which he imagined. He lies for hours imagining this betrayal, reconstructing the scenes in every minute detail, until he goes nearly crazy believing it. His jealousy was really infernal, suffocating, blind, not knowing where to strike and without any reality to support it. A continuous state of doubt. At the end of the day I was shattered. It seemed to me that whatever was in me was awakened in these people and that I was only awakening things which ought better to be left asleep. I was increasing the awareness of pain, and breaking down all defenses against it. Yes, I know they are false defenses, but they are at least as good as the stones over a tomb. They give the illusion that the dead cannot return. But I do not even leave the stone. I take away the symbol of the burial. And that's not all. The next day I awakened with anguish, with a kind of fear. A nameless fear. A kind of universal doubt. I doubted everything. Above all Lilith. I feared to know, to know really what she felt. I would have given my life then to lose all my lucidity. And all day, all day the cripples talked to me about fear. I asked them questions I never asked before. *Describe what you fear most.* They exposed so many fears. But as I asked them it was like asking myself, and awakening my own fears. Fear. The whole world is based on fear, even behind the jealousy of the day before lay fear. Fear of being alone, fear of being abandoned, fear of life, fear of being trapped in tragedy, fear of the animal in us, fear of one's hatred, of committing a crime, fear of cancer, of syphilis, of starvation. I asked myself: was it the fear in me which uncovered all this? It was like opening tombs again. It was *contagion*, Djuna, I tell you. . . . Today I don't know whether this is a healing or a contagion. I am only discovering that we are all alike, and my patients desperately do not want me to be like them."

Djuna walked slowly after leaving Lilith. The day was softer and the snow was melting under her feet. She felt in love with everyone, in love with the whole city. She remembered the tendrils of wild hair on Lilith's neck, and she felt herself inside of Lilith, burning with the cold fire which devoured her. She heard again her voice charged with secret pain, a voice wet with tears passing through a wide mouth made for laughter, a wide, laughing mouth, avid and animal.

She felt the restlessness of the Voice, sitting and listening all day, pinned to his confessions, disguised by the anonymity of vision, and desiring to play an active, personal role in these scenes perpetually unfolding before him. Too near, everything was too near. She felt the multiple footsteps of those walking along with her, not like a march, but like a symphony. In the shock of feet against the pavements she felt the whole collision and impact of human being against human being. They resounded in her. Everything resounded in her. She smiled, thinking of what an immense music box she was. The relation between music and living was not merely an image. What a clear connection between the sound box of instruments and the body, and what sameness between the caresses of the hands! Djuna felt at once so aroused that it was unbearable. She felt all her loves at once, maternal, fraternal, sensual, mystical. So many loves! What was she? The lover of the world? Crazed with love, with remembrance of every touch and flavor, of every caress and word. And simultaneously with the communion, this communion with eyes closed, this taste of the wafer on her tongue, this sonorousness in her ears, this constant simoon wind burning inside of her, came the pain of separation again. When people came as near as this, and breaths were so confounded and confused, then Djuna knew she was possessed.

In the morning the body had been clear like a statue, and as cool. The body moved with the harmony of its form, it stood in altitude, like the spire of a cathedral, it was light and free and passed through the moments easily like the wind, feeling neither doors nor walls nor anger. There was in it the tranquillity of depths, of what lay below the level of storms. It was a mountain asleep without fire in its bowels. It lay asleep as it arranged itself, it moved in accord with its own pattern, with an even tread.

It was the moment of silence. The day begun in crystal clearness was blurred by the ascension of blood passing through the cells. The blood rising through the body like the sap in the trees. Antique vases filled with wine.

Djuna stopped walking. Everything had come too near, too near. The cells were full to overflowing with the warm invasion. The moon was shining hypnotically round, a fixed stare, and all the taboos which held the body upright were dissolved by this stare of the moon calling the blood to its own circle. The moon was circling now inside her body, with the same rhythm. Djuna lost her face, her name. She was tied to the moon by long threads of red tangled blood. She moved like a woman tied to the moon, in a space so vast, pushed by a rhythm so strong that the small woman in her was lost. The moon enveloped her and it opened her to an absolute night without dawn.

Before the storm in her there was a suspense, there was time for fear. The trees were afraid, the sky was breathless, the air rarified, the earth parched.

Now her heart was no longer a heart, it was a drum beating continuously. The skin of her body was stretched like a drum. The tips of her hair were no longer hair, but electric wires charged with lightning. The hair was linked to lightning, the heart was a drum; the skin was a fruit skin exposed to warmth and cold.

The blood was rising and drowning the smaller world of the woman, a curtain of red falling over the eyes, drowning pity. Her tongue lashed like a whip, her voice whirled like a simoon wind, her hands tore everything apart breaking all bonds with man, father, son, lover, brother. Her body was filled with drumming fever, with a delirium. Djuna was in a jungle, alone with her storm. She was alone in the forest of her delirium. Desire leaping wild and blind. The human eyes were closed. The storm was panting in her, the moon smiled, her anger seemed immense like the space around her. An enormous fury, as of an animal long taunted, so that when the blood rose every word withheld, every act of yielding, erupted. She trusted no one as she drank alone in the jungle of desire. Her nails were longer, tearing apart everything she had lulled. The storm of blood brought a cloudburst of laughter, the lightning struck down

115

the love, broke all the bondages, drowned the pity. Djuna was one with the moon, thrusting hands made of roots into the storm, while her heart beat like a drum through the orgy of the moonstorm.

Lilith talking to the Voice. Lilith had a headache.

"My father had headaches like this, and he went mad. Do you think I will go mad? I dream of being under ether and I awake in terror. My father's madness started with headaches. He began slowly to lose his memory. But I kept thinking—perhaps my father is not mad, but has had a dream. This dream has come and installed itself in his life. The dream *is* his life. What was this dream? Could I understand it? If I could see it, share it with him, enter his world and stay in it, perhaps he would not go mad. I feel that madness is only solitude. You only go mad when you see something no one else sees. There is a moment before madness when a person has not yet cut the cord of connection and at this moment someone can hold him back. It's what you do every day. There was the dream of the man who ate flowers so that the war might not come! He was locked up . . . only because he got confused with the symbol, he lived in the symbol. But if you understand it, nothing is mad. Everything is a dream, but we don't always know the meaning. I wanted to know my father's fantasy but he enclosed himself in it. I only discovered it when it was too late."

At night Lilith could not sleep. She lay tangled, restless. Lilith who found the absolute only in fragments, in multiplicity. Remembering the eagerness of the Voice with his finger pointing: "You see? You see? That is what it means. You live in the myth." She lived in the myth. And she was lost in it. Always bathing in a world much larger than other people's, the world of dreams. Always caught again in a whirl, a quest, a continuous, diabolical quest of an absolute that does not flow serenely but is pursued and grasped by sheer wakefulness. In flight always, and she fearing to sleep for fear of its passing. Desire unexploded in her, with the fuse lit and the little flames running up and down with Dyonisian joy; the little flames running around the heart of the dyamite and never touching it. The little flames kept her breathless, nerves bristling with their heads up, necks stretched, thirsty eyes, peaked ears, all the little nerves waiting for the orgasm that will send the blood running through them like an anesthetic and put them to sleep.

Lilith, lying sleepless, seeing in the yellow faces at the bar the faces of future crimes, drug addicts who with knife or poison would bring a kind of sleep, a pause, a rest from this pursuit of a fugitive absolute. Lilith wishing for the crime, the drug, the death, the deliverance. But the nerves are still awake, waiting for the pause of sleep or death, waiting for the dynamite to explode, for the past to crumble, waiting for an absolute uncapturable. Do all violent fires have a hundred flames pointing in all directions, was there ever one round flame with one tongue? Why did this force which did not erupt in quicksilver through the veins, why did it rush out in a typhoon whirl to round up the monsters walking through the streets, to question their intentions, to imagine their perversities, to slide between the foam of lust, between the most knotted and twisted desires? This man with his little girl, why were his eyes so wet, his mouth so wet, why were her eyes so tired, why was her dress so short, her glance so oblique? Why was that young man so white? There was the scum of veronal on his lips. Why did that woman wait under the lamplight with her hand in her muff? This force which did not explode in Lilith was a poison; it spilled into the streets, ran into the gutters. She wanted to be dismembered and devoured but she encountered always wings, eyes opening on the heavens, flames turning to the mystic blue of the night lamps in convents and hospitals.

In Lilith the seed would not burst; the body left the earth, pulled upward by a string of nerves and spilled its pollen only in space, because the fairy tale wore too light a gown, a gown that made a breeze, a space between feet and earth. Lilith's footsteps would soon not be heard and her blood would turn to quicksilver, blue like the night flames of places where people weep.

Lilith entered Djuna's room tumultuously, throwing her little serpent-skin bag on the bed, her undulating scarf on the desk, her gloves on the bookshelf, and talking with fever and excitement: "I'm falling in love with the Voice. I feel he is like a soul detective, and that the day he captures me, I will love him."

"It's a mirage," said Djuna.

She knew that Lilith was pursuing another mirage: the love of the Voice for what the Voice said to her, because the Voice reached into the roots of her being.

"A mystical illusion," repeated Djuna. "A mirage. You know what happens to a woman when she pursues a mirage, if she has a love affair with a mirage?"

"What can happen to her? It's poetry."

"It may be poetry, Lilith, but her nature revolts against it. At some moment or other your body will revolt because it's not real."

"But it is only in his presence that I feel true, natural."

"But don't get any closer to him; If you come closer you will defeat you own salvation. But then . . . you are too lovely, he won't let you pass without making an effort to retain you. That is what happened to me. I lost the father in him—because I wanted to. I tempted him as a man, and when he became a man and desired me, then I was angry at him, as if it had been only a test, a test of the savior in him. And he is no savior. He is trying to save himself too. I liked upsetting him. Then when he became a man and ran after me I was very angry—it seemed to prove that he was only human."

"The world is very small, Djuna. If what you say is true it is very small. I'm going to choke in it. He can't be merely human. He must be something else, something more. He has a magic power."

Lilith enveloped Djuna in great softness. They lay talking in the dark. Only the softness, only to feel the softness and warmth of woman, the weight of her arm, the curve of her neck. Only to hear her breathing and talking and laughing in the dark. To lie there, wishing perhaps to be a man for a moment, but as a woman knowing there is no other way of possessing a woman but as a man.

"Try and close your eyes, you'll find another world that is immense at night, Lilith."

"I never remember the night. Why don't I find a man who makes me feel what I feel with you? You are so warm, you are so quick. You are always where I am. Our impulses towards each other happen at the same moment. You are never late or slow or indifferent, and you have the gift of gesture. When I feel anguished, lost, alone, you always have the gift for saying what I need to hear. After we are together you write me letters, and I need so much to feel what we said, to be able to touch the words. It's the only thing I believe in, Djuna, everything else is ghostly. You say everything with your body, like a dancer. All your body talks, your hands, your walk. I believe you."

"But none of this is love, Lilith. We are the same woman. There is always the moment when all the outlines, the differences between women disappear, and we enter a world where all feelings, yours and mine, seem to issue from the same source. We lose our separate identities. What happens to you is the same as what happens to me. Listening to you is not entering a world different from my own, it's a kind of communion."

"And meanwhile everybody laughs, jeers, and calls us all kinds of names."

What softness between women. The marvelous silences of twinship. To turn and watch the rivulets of shadows between the breasts, to lie on the down of the bed sleeping over one's own body, like sleeping in the forest at night. The marvelous silence of woman's thoughts, the secret and the mystery of night and woman become air, sun, water, plant. Feel the roots resting in the soil, the feet well planted in the coolness, in the brown pressure, firm against this creamy wall of earth. When you press against the body of the other you feel this joy of the roots compressed, sustained, enwrapped in its brownness, with only the seeds of joy stirring. A pleasure ebbing back and forth. Sun pressing luxuriantly against the body. Mystery and coolness of darkness between the four walls of another's flesh. The back of Lilith, this soft, musical wall of flesh, the being floating in the waves of silence, enclosed by the presence of what can be touched. No more falling into space. No more quest, anxiety, seeking, yearning, turning within this compact wall of tender flesh. Touch the delicate tendrils of hair, you touch moss and an end to hunger. This hand holds a strand of hair, the world complete, reduced, in the palm of the hand. You have entered from the dissonances of the street, from the separate, hard fragments walking without legs or head or arms, always mutilated, into the immense vault of an organ chant. Djuna lay at the center of the wheel. Lilith warm and near. The earth turns with a chant of roundness, fullness. It turns into a smooth, full round of plenitude. The spokes pass fast and are not seen at this moment. Only the drunkenness of rotation. Other

119

days the wheel slows down and one gets caught in the spokes. One falls between them, they cut and mangle one. You are caught. The rhythm is broken, you dangle, you are mutilated.

"I never noticed," said Lilith to the Voice, "that the sun comes into this room. I always felt it was a dark room because of all the secrets."

"Perhaps it is in you there are no more secrets."

"I don't know. Your understanding saved me from pain and confusion. I feel dependent on you. You have the vision. I get lost. You teach, you are humanly tender and protective. Do you really think a woman can find her way alone, completely alone?"

"In the world of feeling, yes, but not in the world of interpretation."

"I don't mind my dependence on your interpretations."

"Do you know the meaning of your name? It's the unmated woman, the woman who cannot be truly married to any man, the one whom man can never possess altogether. Lilith, you remember, was born before Eve and was made of red clay, not of human substance. She could seduce and ensorcell but she could not melt into man and become one with him. She was not made of the same substance."

"Do you think I am altogether like the first Lilith?" she asked without looking at him.

"I don't know. The way you talk about dependence does not mean love. It means the love for the father, who is the symbol of God. You are seeking a father. . . ."

What she read in his eyes was the immense pleading of a man, imprisoned inside a seer, calling out for the life in her, and at the very moment when every cell inside her body closed to the desire of the man she saw a mirage before her as clearly as men saw it in the desert, and this mirage was a figure taller than other men, a type of savior, the man nearest to God, whose human face she could no longer see except for the immense hunger in the eyes. And she felt a kind of awe, which she recognized. Every time she was faced with a sacrifice of the self, with the demand of another, a hunger, a prayer, a need, there came this joy. It was like the joy of a prisoner who finds

120

the bars of his cell suddenly broken down. The mirage took the place of all actual physical sensation. It was as if all the walls, all the limitations, all the personal desires were transcended. It was not an ecstasy of the body, but a sudden break with the body, a liberation and a stepping into a new region. With the abandon came this joy as of a transcendent flight upward, breaking the chains of awareness. Abandon brought a drunkenness, the fever of generosity, the joy of self-forgetting. A joyous victim, a victim of imperfections of the universe which it was in her power for the moment, to redress, to alter. In her power, for the moment, to make all the gifts promised long ago by the fairy tales. What usually prevented the fairy tales from materializing was the lack of faith and the lack of love. Human life at this moment seemed the unreal and miniature city, with too many boundaries, too many laws. Giving was the only flight in space permitted to human beings.

While the Voice who was no longer the Seer talked, what she saw was a dark-skinned mythological crab, the cavernous sorrows of the monkey, the agedness of the turtle, the tenderness of the kangaroo, the facile humility of the dog.

In the Voice she felt the ugliness of tree roots, of the earth, and this terrific dark, mute knowing of the animal, for though he was the one most aware of what happened inside others he was the one least aware of what happened in himself. It was too near. He could read the myths and man's dreams but not his own soul. He did not know that the man in him had been denied. He was begging to be made man. The man had been buried within the sage. He had grown old, withered, without having fulfilled his life on earth. That is what his eyes were begging for: a life on earth.

It was a father she was looking for, not a lover.

He said: "With you one travels so far away from reality that it is necessary to buy a return ticket."

She liked him better serious than laughing. He did not know how to laugh. His pranks were pranks of the mind, his humor, paradox, the reversal of ideas. He had not learned what she had learned: not to clutch at the perfume of flowers, not to touch the dew, not to tear all the curtains down, to let exaltation and breath rise, vanish. The perfume of the hours distilled only in silence, the heavy perfume of mysteries untouched by human fingers. The friction of words generated only pain and division. He had not learned to formulate without destroying, without tampering, without withering. An awe of the senses.

His understanding was infinite, like a sea, but Lilith was sailing on it alone. He was everywhere, immense, but not a man, because his understanding ended where the life of silence and mystery began.

He was walking at Lilith's side now in full daylight. His clothes hung about him as on a cross of wood. They did not dress him, make him incarnate. His small hands made brusque gestures as if made of bones. Clothes take the shape of a man's body, of his gestures. They bear the imprint of his character, his habits, his moods. The hat reveals if he is mellow and tolerant, if he is gay or lavish. Every line, fold, wrinkle, testifies to his tenderness or roughness, his sensuality or asceticism.

The Voice's clothes did not fit him, were never a part of him. They were not molded by his body, kneaded to his moods. Nothing that men wore seemed to be made for him. The tailors had not cut for his body, his body was not made for clothes. His hat stood stiffly detached from him. It seemed either too large or too small for him. Either his hats were formal and the face under them too lax, or the hat was humorous and nonchalant and his face too serious and heavy. Or else he looked humiliated. In every detail his clothes were a misfit. The body was denied: it did not flow into the clothes, espouse them. There was a kind of blight upon his body; it was the idea made flesh, the idea always standing in the way of natural gestures, the idea upright and standing in the way of rhythm. His flesh was the color of death. He had died in the body and never been resurrected. Heavy with melancholy, jealousy. The life of the mind had shriveled the body too soon. It was a sad flesh tyrannized by the idea, drawn and quartered on a pattern, devoured by concepts. No matter how clear or divine the soul was, the flesh was dark and sad and muddied like the very ancient flesh exiled from joy and faith to the kingdom of thought.

When they returned from the theater or a dance and stood before her door there was always a pause. The Voice would say: "Come and talk with me awhile longer. I hate to surrender you to sleep."

If she refused she would find a note under her door the next day:

"You belong to the night. I have to give you up to the night, to your mystery." She smiled. Her mystery was so simple, but he could not understand it.

The next day he wrote her a long letter and slipped it under her door. Tied to it was a diminutive frog. "This," he wrote, "is my transformation, to permit my entrance through the closed door."

But this diminutive frog she held in the palm of her hand resembled him so much that it made her weep. Indeed the frog had come just as in the fairy tales; and just as in the fairy tales, she must keep her faith and her inner vision of him, must keep on believing in what lay hidden in this frog's body. She must pretend not to notice that the Voice was born disguised, to test her love. If she kept her inner vision the disguise might be destroyed, the metamorphosis might occur.

She sat on the floor with the letter in her lap and the frog in the palm of her hand, weeping over his ugliness and humility and the faith she must retain.

She was asking him questions about his childhood. He stopped in the middle of a story to weep. "Nobody ever asked me anything about myself. I have listened to the confessions of others for twenty-five years. No one has ever turned and asked me about myself, has ever let me talk. No one has ever tried to divine my moods or needs. There are times, Lilith, when I wanted so much to confess to someone. I was filled with preoccupations. Do you know what I fear most in the world? To be loved as a father, a doctor. And it is always so I am loved."

She used his own formulas against him. When he complained that she left him alone she gave him mysterious explanations: that the reality of living always brought tragedy, that she preferred the dream. The Voice was forced to admit gallantly that he preferred the dream. The explanations enchanted and eluded him and saved her from saying: "I don't want you near me because I don't love you."

His concern with the accuracy of the psychological interpretations was so great that once, after the discovery that she had lied to him (he thought he had cured her of lying) he said: "Let me solve this thing alone. Don't bother about details of any kind. What do our personal lives matter when the whole man-made world is at stake?"

The only joy she experienced was that of being completely understood, justified, absolved in all but her relationship to him. He always asked her what she had been doing. No matter what she told him, even about the trivial purchase of a bracelet, the Voice pounced upon it with excitement and raised the incident to a complete, dazzling, symbolical act, a part of a legend. The little incident was all he needed to compose and complete this legend. The bracelet had a meaning—everything had a meaning. Every act revealed more and more clearly this divine pattern by which she lived and of which the Voice alone knew the entire design. Now he could see. He repeated over and over again: "You see? You see?" Lilith had the feeling that she had been doing extraordinary things. When she stepped into a shop and bought a bracelet it was not, as she thought, because of the love of its color or its shape, or because she loved adornment. She was carrying in herself at that moment the entire drama of woman's slavery and dependence. In this obscure little theater of her unconscious the denouement brought about by the purchase of the bracelet was a drama which had everlasting repercussions on her daily life. It signified the desire to be bound to someone, it expressed a desire to yield. You see? You see? Not only was the bracelet or the lovely moment spent before the shop window magnified and brought into violent relief—as an act full of implications, of repercussions—but all she had done during the week seemed to open like a giant hothouse camellia whose growth had been forced by a travail of creation from the moment she first drew breath.

While the Voice tracked down each minor incident of her life to expose the relation between them, the fatality and importance of the link between them, the heavy destined power of each one, she felt like an actress who had never known how moving she had been, she felt like a creator who had prepared in some dim laboratory of her soul a life like a legend, and only today could she read the legend itself out of an enormous book.

This was part of the legend, this little man brusquely deciphering each incident, marveling ever at the miracle which had never seemed a miracle before, her walking along and buying a bracelet, as miraculous to the Voice as lead turning to gold in an alchemist's bottle. She had not only covered the earth with a multitude of spontaneous acts but these acts accomplished so slidingly, so swiftly, could all be illumined with spiritual significance, divine intentions, loved for their human quality or feared for their uniqueness. He worshiped them for the very act of their flowering.

He revolted now and then against her uncapturableness, but she subtilized the situation. She did not want reality. She feared reality. She was really a flame. No one could possess a flame. She annulled the boundaries, confused the issues. All the definite decisions, outlines, realities, she melted into a dreamlike substance. She enchanted him, hypnotized him with inventions and creations, so that he would cease his clutching, become cosmic again. She talked him out of the reality of her presence.

What he did not know was that at the same time she was losing her faith in all interpretations, since she saw how they could be manipulated to conceal the truth. She began to feel the illusory quality of all man's interpretations, and to believe only in her feelings. Every day she found in mythology a new pretext for eluding his desire for her. First she needed time. She must become entirely herself and without need of him. She was waiting for the moment when she would have no need of him as a doctor. She was waiting for the man and the doctor to become entirely separate and never to be again confused in her. This he accepted.

But when he was not being the doctor, she discovered, he was not a man but a child. He wept like a child, he raged, he was filled with fears, he was possessive, he complained and lamented about himself, his own life. He was desperately hungry and awkward in life, clutching rather than enjoying. The human being hidden in the healer was stunted, youthful, hysterical. As soon as he ceased to be a teacher and a guide, he lost all his strength and deftness. He was disoriented, chaotic, blind. As soon as he stepped out of his role he collapsed. Lilith found herself confronting a child lamenting, regretting, impatient, fretful, lonely. He wrote inchoate love notes with ink blots, he leaped to meet her in the street, perspiring and nervous. He was jealous of the man who washed her hair. The child that she awakened in him was like the child in those who had come to him for care, unsatisfied, lamenting, tearful, sickly. Neither her powers of illusion nor her dreams had worked the miracle. He remained nothing but A VOICE.

Awareness hurts. Relationships hurt. Life hurts. But to float, to drift, to live in the dream does not hurt. Her eyes were closing. She was drifting, drifting. Drunkenness. It was not the Hotel Chaotica which had many rooms, but she, Djuna, when she lay on her bed, folding them all together, the layers and all the things that she was not yet.

When I entered the dream I stepped on a stage. The lights cast on it changed hue and intensity like stage lights. The violent scenes happened in the spotlight and were enveloped by a thick curtain of blackness. The scenes were cut, interrupted, or broken with entr'actes. *The* mise en scéne *was stylized, and only what has meaning was represented. And very often I was at once the victim and observer.*

The dream was composed like a tower of layers without end, rising upward and losing themselves in the infinite, or layers coiling downward, losing themselves in the bowels of the earth. When it swooped me into its undulations, the spiraling began, and this spiral was a labyrinth. There was no vault and no bottom, no walls and no return. But there were themes repeating themselves with exactitude.

If the walls of the dream seemed lined with moist silk, and the contours of the labyrinth lined with silence, still the steps of the dream were a series of explosions in which all the condemned fragments of myself burst into a mysterious and violent life, with the heavy maternal solicitude of the night ever attentive to their flowering.

On the first layer of the spiral there was awareness. I could still see the daylight between the fringe of eyelashes. I could still see the interstices of the world. This was the penumbra, where the thoughts were inlaid in filaments of lightning. It was the place where the images were delicately filtered and separated, and their silhouettes thrown against space. It was the place where footsteps left no trace, where laughter had no echo, but where hunger and fear were immense. It was the place where the sails of reverie could swell while no wind was felt.

The vegetation no longer concealed its breathing, its lamentations. The sand no longer concealed its desire to enmesh, to stifle; the sea showed its true face, its insatiable craving to possess; the earth yawned open its caverns, the fogs spewed out their poisons. The dream was full of danger like the African jungle. The dream was full of animals. All the animals killed, stuffed, imprisoned by man, walked alive in the dream. The faces mocked all desire to identify, to personalize: they changed and decomposed before my eyes.

There was no time: events passed without leaving a trace, a footprint, an echo. They left SPACE around them. Even a crowded street lay perpendicular between two abysses, as if it belonged to a planet without gravitation.

The dream was a filter. The entire world was never admitted. It was a stage surrendered to fragments, with many pieces left hanging in shreds.

At the tip of the spiral I felt passive, felt bound like a mummy. As I descended these obstacles loosened.

The loss of memory was like the loss of a chain. With all this fluidity came a great lightness. Without memory I was immensely light, vaporous, fluid. The memory was the density which I could not transcend except in the dream.

I was not lost, I had only lost the past. Sand passing through the hourglass which never turned. Passing.

When the dream fell to one side, wounded, and the daytime into another, what appeared through the crack was the real death. The crack of daylight between the curtains, the slit between night and day was the mortal moment for it killed the dream. The soul then lost its power to breathe, lost its space.

Nights when I awaited the dream, as one awaits the ship that is to take one far away, and the nightmare came in its place, then I knew that I had something to expiate. The nightmare was the messenger of guilt. The nightmare brought me whatever suffering I had rejected or eluded during the day or given to others.

Now it was not altogether the dream nor was it the daylight. It was the moment when one was awake with a million eyes and a mouth that had said everything and was now struck with silence; a place so high that breathing ceased and divination began.

It was the twilight of mercury. It was here that everything happened to me. The daytime was only a sketch. In the daytime all the gestures were

127

thickened by remembrance. Only in the dream was the loved one wholly possessed, only in the dream was there ecstasy without death. Life began only behind the curtain of closed eyelashes.

The woman who walked erect during the day and the woman who breathed and walked and swam during the night were not the same. The day woman was like a cathedral spire, and the opening into her being was a secret. It was inaccessible like the tip of the most labyrinthian sea shell.

But with the night came the openness.

The day body made of rigid bones, made rigid with fears and dissonances, was set against yielding. At night it changed substance, form and texture. With the night came fluidity. With the night there ran through the marrows not only blood which could commingle with other bloods, but a mercury which ran in all directions, swift, mordant, uncontrollable, spilling and running in star points, changing shape at each breath of desire, spilling and dispersing without separating.

With the night came space. No crowded city. The dream was never crowded. It was filtered through the prism of creation. The pressure of time ceased. Joy lasted longer and suffering less, or else all the feelings were telescoped into a second. Time was arranged and ordained by feeling. Fear was eternal, anger immediate and catastrophic. Sifted and enveloped in a mineral glow, each object of the eternal landscape appeared on the scene with space around it. The space was like an enormous silence in which there was no sword of thought, no rending comments, no thread ever cut. I walked among symbols and silence.

I ceased to be a woman. The secret small pores of the being began to breathe a life of plant and flower. I went to sleep a human being and awakened with the nervous sensibility of a leaf, with the fin-knowledge of fish, with the hardness of coral, with the sulphurous eyes of a mineral. I awakened with eyes at the end of long arms that floated everywhere and with eyes on the soles of my feet. I awakened in strands of angel hair with lungs of cocoon milk.

With the night came a multiplied breathing and new cells like honeycombs filled with a strange activity. Filling and refilling with white tides and red currents, with echoes and fever. Cells, beehives of feelings, inundated with new forms of life dissolving the outline of the body. All forms became blurred and the woman who was lying there slowly turned into a heavy sea, carrying riches on her breast, or became earth with many fissures of thirst, drinking rain.

128

CPSIA information can be obtained
at www.ICGtesting.com
Printed in the USA
LVOW07s0923031216
515425LV00002BA/2/P